To My B—

En to this pm. I really appreciate your support and friendship. You are a true asset to any one you come in contact with.

God Bless!

Your boy

Brooklyn

SAVANNAH

SAVANNAH

By
Brooklen Borne

Bee 5ive Productions
In association with
Firestorm Publication

Bee 5ive Productions
3020 Wexford Walk Dr
Smyrna, GA. 30080
Bee5pinc@gmail.com

"Savannah"

Copyright © 2007 by Brooklen Borne

Cover Photo by: Mr. Derrick Henry of DDMC Photography
Front Cover Graphics by: Ms. Leslie Taylor
Cover Model: Ms. Anetral Hall
Back Cover Graphics by: Mr. Karl "The Pathfinder" Anthony
Author Photo by: Portrait Innovations

This book is a work of fiction. All rights reserved. No part of this book may be reproduced or transmitted in any form or by any means, electronic or mechanical, including photocopying and recording, or by any information storage and retrieval system, without permission in writing from the publisher.

ISBN 10: 0615489737
ISBN 13: 978-0615489735

Printed in the United States of America

Dedicated

To those who are trying to get their stories told and those who gave them the opportunity to do so.

-Brooklen Borne

Acknowledgments

First and foremost, I would like to give thanks to my Heavenly Father above for blessing me with the ability to bring my words to life, by putting my thoughts on paper.

I would like to thank all those who have supported me on my anticipated journey in the literary world. Words can't express what this means to me. Thank you so much.

I am indebted to **Jackie Seaton, Anetral Hall, Degala Blalock, Lushanna Thompson, Tetsuko Hasegawa, Joyah Seaton, Lashann Lunnon, Christina Hackett, Tina Harris, Daneille Johnson, Diane Johnson** and **Evelyn Read.**

Last, but not least, I am grateful to all the wonderful people who kept me motivated and inspired during my work on this project.

SAVANNAH WHO?
By LuShanna Thompson

Savannah who, you ask?
What's in a name anyway?
Does it define who I am? Where I've been? Who I've seen or who I've become?
My beauty, so sweet and innocent, is what you can see with your eyes.
A soft tone whisper is what blows in your ear.
Too bad you didn't look deeper into the pupils of my light brown eyes.
Then you would have noticed the pain and deep hatred I bare.
Words can't come close to who I am.
I'm Bonnie, damn the Clyde!
I'm Thelma and Louise.
You dare touch the thin air of my silence?
I overcame sorrow and despair, not to mention the physical healing.
It will take more than what you've thrown at me to keep me down.
I'm your mother, your sister, your lover, your friend, your neighbor, or maybe your enemy.
Dare ask who!
I'm **Savannah** Carrington.
I thought you knew!

Have you ever had a day, when everything was going well and it gave you the sense this is the way life is suppose to be? Then all of a sudden, someone enters your world and in an instant, screws it all up?

Brooklen Borne

CHAPTER ONE
"He moved her thong to the side"

Thank God it's Friday, Savannah Carrington mumbled to herself, as she walked toward the parking lot to meet up with the van pool, to take her back to her peaceful home in Settle Woods; a subdivision in Waldorf, Maryland. Waldorf is about twenty minutes away from downtown DC and is considered Washington's suburbia. She was about to open the door to the van when her cell phone began to vibrate. Thinking to herself as she fumbled through her bag, *this better not be work, because they will get cursed out; if they're trying to call me back into the office.* She answered, never looking at the caller ID.
"Hello."
"This is your loving husband."
"Hey baby, what's up?" Savannah responded, relieved it wasn't her job.
"You've been working hard all week honey and since its Friday, we're going to have a special evening; so don't take the van pool. I'm coming to pick you up and we're going to spend some quality time together away from the kids. My parents are picking them up as we speak."
"Hmm . . . that sounds naughty."
"Naughty only by our own nature, baby."
"Marcus, you're so crazy."
"I'm five minutes away."
"Alright, see you then."
Savannah worked as an analysis for a contracting company located on Boling Air Force Base. The base is located on the edge of Washington, DC and she really enjoyed working there. Her first day on the job, she had to let her co-workers and boss know that she is a loyal person and will give them a hundred and ten percent, but don't expect her to kiss anybody's ass; and don't try to play her for a

Savannah

fool. Five years later no one has cross those lines and that's why she is still there and loving it.

When Marcus arrived he greeted her with a kiss, two dozen long stem roses, and told her he was taking her to the Capital Grille restaurant; on Pennsylvania Avenue, in downtown D.C. Never one to shy away from showing his love, he always had a surprise for her. He treats her like a Queen, twenty-four seven. As they left the base and made their way onto the highway, he raised her semi short black skirt and placed his right hand on her left inner thigh and began to massage, while the blade of his hand gently glided up and down the entrance of her kitty; as they veered onto the 395 towards downtown. Now with a wet pussy, swollen lips and a protruding clit, she needed more than just a hand job and suggest they skip dinner and go home. Ignoring her request he moved her thong to the side and slipped two fingers inside, gently working her clit. With her eyes closed and mouth open breathing hard as if she had asthma, Savannah reached for anything she could grasp as she came instantly. She was in pure bliss as she yelled, "Damn baby!"

Marcus placed his fingers in his mouth and licked them clean of her juices and said, "Thank you baby for the appetizer." Her only response was to lick her lips and place her hand over her face; as she squeezed her thighs together. Although his fingers were no longer exploring her sugar walls, she continued to have short burst of pleasurable orgasmic waves as they flowed throughout her body. Trying desperately to regain control of herself before they reached the restaurant.

Marcus smiled as he rested his hand back on her thigh and drove on. It's a good thing the windows were darkly tinted, otherwise she would have given the other motorist a silent movie show.

*****

They arrived back home around nine. The kids were with Marcus's parents and they were going to take full advantage of their quality time alone. Marcus had just stepped out the shower and was drying himself off, when Savannah walked passed him to get in. He stopped her in her tracks, and reached for her arm and gently pulled her closer to him. Her hands explored his sculptured chest as he began kissing her on the neck. Her nipples were at full attention as if they were in the Marine Corps, and he took full advantage of them. His tongue played with them ever so softly. The sensation felt like velvet against her skin. His touch was very sensual, and the exclusive area between her legs became moist like Duncan Hines. She leaned against the wall placing one leg on top of the sink counter and the other on the floor for balance, hinting to him that she was ready to be filled by his thickness; when he suddenly stopped and told her. "When you come out the shower, I'll be in the bed waiting for you baby." Savannah could have knocked him the hell out.

"Marcus! I don't believe you got me all hot and worked up, and didn't finish the act. That's not right baby! That's just not right!" she said biting her bottom lip and frowning. He just winked at her and tapped her on her booty as she entered the shower.

Ten minutes later she emerged feeling refreshed and began drying off. Slow sultry music could be heard coming from the bedroom, and the more she dried her body, the hornier she became. She reached on the sink counter for the Amber Romance body spray, from Victoria Secret and gave herself a quick spray over. She entered the bedroom wearing nothing but her birthday suit. She was ready.

The room was illuminated by the fire place and scented candles. The rose petals on the floor formed a walkway leading to the bed. Marcus was lying on the bed with the sheets turned back, holding two glasses of champagne. She walked over to him and took one of the glasses. They toasted and drank the contents, before placing the empty glasses on the night stand. As the champagne began to take its toll, she was beyond ready to please her man. She eased onto the bed and crawled toward her man like a Panther sneaking upon its prey. She gently took a hold of his baby maker and started sucking on it like a Popsicle on a hot summer's day. He began to massage her head with every bob as her tongue slowly continued to explore the length of his shaft.

Savannah

"Damn, baby! Your mouth is lethal." He moaned. He then reached for her shoulders, to reposition her over his mouth as they got in the sixty-nine position. He began sucking and licking her clit, while firmly squeezing her round booty. She held onto the edge of the bed with one hand for leverage, while keeping a steady stroke on his shaft with the other. *Damn, this man has me turned out*, she thought to herself. She lived for his touch. The things that Marcus was doing to her southern hemisphere were driving her to ecstasy. Savannah began grinding on his mouth like a woman possessed. She was so wet; her juices were trickling down the side of his mouth. Her clit was being entertained by his chin, while her kitty was getting worked by his tongue and her asshole being stimulated by his middle finger like a vibrator. After five minutes of such intense attention, she turned around and slid his hard sex organ inside her. She rode him as if she was on a mechanical bull, while he massaged her breast and nipples. Her nipples were so hard you could have hung a framed picture from them.

"Oh, yes! I'm about to cum, baby!" she screamed, as she fucked him like a hooker on 'Spanish Fly. 'She yelled out his name as her hips began moving rapidly back and forth against his pelvis.

"Ooh baby, I'm coming." She blurted out, as her juices flowed down his shaft and around his balls coming to a rest on the silk sheets. A few humps later, she collapsed on top of him. Breathing heavily, she looked at him. "You did mommy right." He placed his hand on the left side of her face and began to tongue her down. He rolled her over into the missionary position slowly pouring his hardness inside of her. She dug her nails into his back and threw her hips up to greet his incoming thrusts. He had her sounding like Mariah Carey hitting one of her high notes. Fifteen minutes later of uninterrupted missionary love making and her nail marks all over Marcus's back, she had an orgasm that had her nearly paralyzed.

"Honey, I want you to come now." Savannah pleaded trying to regain control of her body. Her man obliged by positioning her in the doggie style. He took a hold of her hips and began jack hammering her sugar walls. She was balling up the sheets as she bit and screamed into the pillow, with every luscious stroke. She knew he was about to come. He was hitting her G-spot as if he was Derek

Jeter trying to take one out the park. He began to grunt as he buried all seven inches into her love canal. Holding tightly onto her hips, he released their future children deep inside her. She was incoherent as Marcus took her to another level. "Daddy, we've been at it for almost three hours," Savannah managed to say, looking over at the clock exhausted.

"I had to make sure I took care of my woman." Marcus responded.

She leaned toward him and kissed him on his sexy full lips and replied, "And that you did daddy."

Savannah was dozing off in Marcus's arms, when she thought she heard something downstairs. She quickly dismissed the thought, knowing the kids weren't home and the alarm was set. Suddenly Marcus yelled out, "Who the fuck is you and what are you doing in my house?" Startled by his outburst, Savannah looked at Marcus and then in the direction where he was staring. Standing in the doorway, were two figures fully dressed in black. Her heart was pounding. She rose up from the bed wondering *how in the hell they got into her house.* They had installed a top of the line security system two days earlier. Marcus began reaching for his gun that was in the nightstand draw. Without saying a word, the intruders opened fire spraying them with bullets as they scurried for cover. The moment seemed as if it was playing out in slow motion. The muzzles of their guns lit up every time a bullet left the chamber. Glass shattered around them, and Savannah screamed and prayed at the same time. Feathers from the down pillows and comforter filled the air, as the bullets made contact with them. Savannah felt a hot sharp pain rip through her right shoulder knocking her off the bed and onto the floor. She felt another hot sharp pain through her left shoulder, then another in her upper left thigh and two more in her back.

She began gasping for air. Down feathers that once floated in the air, came to a rest all around her. Savannah vision was becoming blurry, when the clock fell in front of her, just missing her face by inches. The soft white digital numbers on the clock read: 12:49. The cordless phone was underneath the bed. She reached for it and somehow managed to dial 9-1-1. She heard the operator ask,

Savannah

"What is the nature of your call?" She couldn't answer. Her fingers slid off the phone as she started to lose consciousness as life began to leave her body.

CHAPTER TWO
"I'll give you ten minutes"

"Mama . . . Mama, wake up. Mama, I love you." Savannah heard her son Devin's voice but she was so sedated, it took her a while before she was able to open her eyes. Her vision slowly came into focus. She saw her four year old standing beside the bed smiling at her. "Gran' ma!" He informed, while pointing at his mother.

Savannah's mother came into view. "Thank You Jesus, for giving me back, my baby."She said with her hands clasped together, before yelling out to Savannah's father. "Irving! Call the doctor, Savannah eyes are open. Hurry! Thank You, Lord Jesus." She repeated once more, while smiling and hugging her grandson, Devin. Savannah could barely open her mouth, as she asked her mother in a whisper, is Marcus alright? Her mother didn't answer. Savannah thought her mother might not have heard her. She was about to ask her again, when a young black doctor, wearing gold wired framed glasses came rushing into the room, with Savannah's father behind him and her son, Chance.

"I am Doctor Yard." He spoke with a slight southern accent, taking out a small flash light and alternated the beam of light in Savannah's eyes. As he checked her vital signs he asked. "How do you feel?" In a whisper, she responded.

"I'm thirsty, and I feel like I've been hit by a Mac truck." The doctor instructed the nurse standing next to him, to bring a cup of ice and a pitcher of water.

"You're lucky to be alive, Mrs. Carrington. You were shot seven times."

"Doctor, where am I and how long have I been here?" She asked still feeling groggy. "You're at Washington Hospital Center, and you've been unconscious for four days." He replied, while checking her blood pressure.

Savannah

"Where's my husband? Is he alright? The doctor looked at her and was about to answer, when the nurse entered the room with Savannah's water and two men wearing suits. The nurse placed the cup of ice and the pitcher of water on the table by the bed, and said to Dr. Yard. "Doctor, these F.B.I. agents would like to talk to Mrs. Carrington." Both men flashed their credentials to the doctor. The taller of the two agents said.
"We need to ask Mrs. Carrington a few questions."

"I'll give you ten minutes. She just came out of a coma and I need to run some more test on her." Dr. Yard informed them as he closed his clip board and departed the room.

"I'm Special Agent Owens, and this is Agent Murray. We would like to ask you a few questions about the shooting at your home. Do you know who shot you and your husband?"

"Where is my husband?"

"Do you know who shot you, Mrs. Carrington?"

"Where is my husband?" Savannah asked again, feeling weak and getting frustrated.

"Could you answer the question, Mrs. Carrington?"

"I don't have a clue who shot me and my husband. All I know is my husband and I was in bed, when two figures dressed in black, stood in the doorway of our bedroom. My husband noticed them and confronted them."

"Do you remember what your husband said to them?"

"He said. Who the fuck is you and what are you doing in my house? They didn't respond. They just opened fire on us."

"Ma'am, do you know if they were black or white, female or male?"

"I just told you. I didn't have a clue. Whoever those people were, they were dressed in black from head to toe. The room was dark and their faces were covered. I couldn't give you a description, if you offered to pay me a million dollars. Look Agent Owens, right now, all I want to know is what happened to Marcus. Can you or somebody in this room tell me what happened to my husband?" Savannah asked as she sat up in the bed, on her elbows. Agent Owens looked down at his department issued memo pad before saying, "Your husband is dead ma'am."

Brooklen Borne

Savannah felt like someone had reached inside her chest and snatched her heart out. As she sank down in the bed, tears began to fall from her eyes like water flowing down a stream. Her mother immediately took the kids out the room. Her father took a hold of her hand. Dr. Yard came back into the room and told the agents, their time was up and they had to leave. As the two agents put away their pads, Agent Owens gave her father his card and told him. "If she remembers anything, anything at all, please give them a call."
Agent Murray then looked over at Savannah and said, "Mrs. Carrington, we're sorry for your loss." Both agents placed their pads back inside their jackets and left the room. Dr. Yard asked Savannah was she alright, but she couldn't answer him. She thought to herself, *how can I be alright and I was just told my husband has been murdered.* Then her body went numb. Her father leaned over and hugged her, as she held on to him for dear life and began to cry out loud. She knew she would never see her husband, who was her best friend ever again. As she cried, she couldn't believe she was experiencing such a nightmare while being awake. *Who would want to invade our home to kill us?* Was the question that kept swirling in her head, giving her a migraine. The more she thought about the question why, the worst she felt the pain. The more she felt the pain, the harder she would cry. The harder she cried, the tighter she held on to her father; because she was very much afraid and alone and didn't know what to do. She loved Marcus, he was her world.

*****

Marcus was a handsome man. Everyone who saw him said he could pass for Brian McKnight's double. Marcus did eight years in the Navy, before he got out and became a fire inspector at North Island, in San Diego. After two years there, he transferred to Bolin Air Force Base, in D.C., doing the same job. He is one of the very few African American fire inspectors in the business. He and Savannah met at Bolin and after being engaged for a year, they got married. Savannah had given the Air Force seven years, before she became tired of the baby sitting game and got out. Watching over grown men and woman handling their problems, they should be able

Savannah

to handle themselves, but couldn't or wouldn't; was becoming too much for her. She now works as an analyst for a government contractor, there on Bolin. She's not in charge of anyone and that's the way she liked it. She's just responsible for the job that she's assigned and at the end of the day, she goes home. Everything was going great in her life and couldn't ask for more. She was truly blessed.

Life as she knew it was picture perfect. She had a beautiful home, a loving husband, two well mannered boys and a job she really looked forward going to everyday. Savannah would never have thought in a million years, her life would change in such a way, that it has. She was daydreaming, these kinds of thing only happens to other people, like on television and the news or in the movies; now she was the news. For the first time in Savannah's life she was truly lost. She was blessed to have her parents and children, but she didn't have her man, her lover, her best friend by her side anymore. She felt so empty, but she had to pull it together for her two sons.

*****

Savannah was still in very bad shape and Doctor Yard wouldn't release her to attend her husband's funeral. He was very apologetic for the decision he had to make; but it was in the best interest of her health and full recovery. She was still hooked up to, too many machines. Her parents had a relative videotaped the service for her. She was so grateful for that. It tore her up inside not to be there, but she knew Marcus spirit would always live in her heart.

Marcus's service was held at Christ Remnants Church of God, located in Temple Hills, Maryland. Her mother told her that Pastor William J. Tucker had spoken some beautiful words about her husband, since he knew her husband from when he was a little boy. He was laid to rest with military honors at Arlington National Cemetery. Her mother informed her Devin was all right during the service. He's so young and don't fully understand what's really going on. Chance was taking it pretty hard because he's older and knows a lot more, despite not knowing all the details, about his mother and his father. Her son is going to remember this for the rest of his life and Savannah prayed that it doesn't affect him in a negative way as he grows to adult hood. Tears and a runny noise dampened her face as she recalls that night, in her head. The fears and the psychological effects of this tragic event have taken its toll on her, her sons and both families.

CHAPTER THREE
"Okay let's get out of here..."

    Ricky Fontayne parents were hard working, law abiding people. They struggled to make ends meet like everyone else in their low income south side Chicago neighborhood. His father would gamble every now and then, to get extra money. One evening, when he and his younger brother Maurice returned home from getting some candy from the corner grocery store, their father was lying on the living room floor in a pool of blood. He had been stabbed in the heart. The boys yelled for their mother, as tears rolled down their little cheeks as they ran toward their parent's bedroom. Their mother also lying in a pool of blood on the bed, apparently had been raped and stabbed several times in her chest and stomach area; but she miraculously survived the attack. Ricky stood at his mother's side and told his brother to call 9-1-1 and their grandmother in Baltimore. Within minutes, the house was filled with emergency personnel.
    The next morning, a Cook county social worker, who was a friend of the family, took the boys to the hospital to visit their mother. Without the boy's knowledge, the hospital suggested they be brought there, because the doctors weren't sure if their mother was going to make it through the night.
    It was a miracle that after all she had gone through; she was able to speak to her children. She was very weak, but her words were strong, clear and to the point. She told Ricky to look after his younger brother. His mother seemed to be getting weaker by the minute but she had a firm grip on his arm and concealed her weakness from him, as she made Ricky promise to what she ask. With tears streaming down the cheeks of both boys, he promised his mother that he would always look out for little Maurice. She hugged and kissed both her babies before they were escorted out the room by a nurse, to wait in the hallway, so the social worker could speak to their mother in private.

Savannah

Mrs. Fontayne informed the social worker that there was a notarized letter between the mattress and box spring of her bed, giving the boy's grandmother custody of her sons, in case anything ever happened to her, and their father. She also informed the social worker that she had some money stashed inside a chicken, in the freezer section of the refrigerator and that should be enough to care for them, until she got out the hospital.

The social worker acknowledged the information and rubbed Mrs. Fontayne hand and wished her a speedy recovery, before turning to leave the room. An hour later Mrs. Fontayne passed away, due to complications from her injuries. A few months later the boys were told by their grandmother what had happened to their parents, the day they found them in the house. Their father had barrowed some money from a local street hustler and wasn't able to pay it back on the agreed date. So the hustler sent some thugs over to the house to send a message. The end result of borrowing a few hundred dollars for a gambling habit resulted in both parents' death, and no one was ever charged for their murder. The sad thing is Mrs. Fontayne had four hundred dollars stashed away, in case of an emergency.

The boy's grandmother was doing a wonderful job, staying on top of the two and keeping them out of trouble. Ricky and Maurice were doing very well in school and they were model students until their grandmother became sick and was no longer able to look after them. She was put in a nursing home, because she needed 24 hour care and the boys were placed into the foster care system. Six months later, the brothers were place in the care of Mr. and Mrs. Lewis, a couple in their late fifties, maybe early sixties that already had two biological sons and another boy from the foster care system, named David Cobb. He was seventeen and had been with them nearly a year. He was street smart beyond his years and was looking forward to his birthday in five months. The truth was they didn't really care about the foster children. All they cared about was the monthly checks they received from the state, and their two biological spoiled and rotten sons. The Lewis's would buy new clothes for their children and the three foster children would get the "hand-me-downs." He was ready to move out and be on his own.

Brooklen Borne

The Lewis's seemed to be very loving and caring to the foster children they cared for. Ricky and Maurice had only been there for two months before their situation changed for the worst and set the path to their future, as adults. David, Ricky and Maurice were in the room listening to music one evening, when the two biological sons burst into the room; each carrying four bags. The three boys were startled as the two began boasting about getting new clothes and began stripping out the clothes they were in and tossing them in the direction of David, Ricky and Maurice; even their dirty underwear.

"Why do you have to disrespect us man?" David asked upset, but keeping his cool.

You really want to know why, because we can!" The older of the two responded, as the younger one laughed and began putting on his new clothes.

Without saying another word, Ricky jumped up and kicked one boy in the temple knocking him out, and before the other boy could react, all three pounced on him and gave him a beat down like he had never experienced. Ricky stood over him and jumped into the air and came down on his leg, breaking it in two places. The boy screamed from the pain as Ricky walked over to the one that was knocked out and did the same to him. He made a low grunt. David and Ricky immediately began packing their clothes; they knew they would be in big trouble once their foster parents arrived home. Maurice then sat on the bed and began to write a letter.

"What are you doing?" David asked with some urgency.

"I'm just writing a quick letter explaining why their two dumb ass sons are laying on the floor with broken legs." Ricky just smiled. "Then I'm going to send one to our social worker, so she knows what's been going on here; just in case these people try to lie on us." Before grabbing their bags, Ricky reached in the boy's pockets and retrieved about five hundred dollars. Then to add insult to injury Maurice unzipped his pants and pissed on them.

"Okay, let's get out of here." Ricky commanded as they picked up their belongings and left. They weren't very far from the house before they decided to split up the money. Once the money was evenly split, they said their good-byes.

Savannah

David went in one direction, and Ricky and Maurice went in another; never to see him again.

Ricky was fourteen and Maurice was twelve, when they were introduced into the street pharmaceutical business by an eighteen-year-old dealer named Charles Monroe a.k.a. "Blue." Blue was given the nickname because of his dark complexion. Slender build but muscular, his hair cut close, and wearing a white wife beater, with sagging' black jeans and a pair of brand new white air force one sneakers, Blue looked like the typical street smart young thug. His upper teeth were platinum with diamonds encrusted on the front two. They sat in a booth at a McDonalds, near the harbor; while Blue recruited them with his best sale pitch. It wasn't too difficult to sell Ricky and Maurice on the street life. They got into the business as a necessity, rather than a want. The little money they had was almost gone and sort to living on the streets wherever they could lay their heads, while staying out of sight from the cops and the Department of Social Services. In his desperation to keep his word and to take care of his little brother, selling drugs instead of going to school seem to be the answer to his dilemma.

After being in the business for about a year, Ricky and Maurice rose quickly up the ranks and earned the reputation as hard working, loyal and tight lipped. It was a warm sunny afternoon, and as they re-upped on their product. Blue let Ricky on, that he was going to put a rival dealer to sleep, so they could expand.

"Man, you crazy. Do you really know who you are talking about taking out?"

"Yeah!" Blue responded with confidence. Our business is thriving, we are feared, and so what's the problem? I know you ain't goin' bitch on me."

"Come on now, you know I don't roll like that. I just don't like the odds and suicide missions are for the military and mutha-fuckas with a death wish."

"Why should we let that niggah make money off our streets and slide his ass back to New York, enjoying the fruit of his labor off our clients?

Brooklen Borne

This mutha-fucka is coming and going as he pleased, like he was born and raised in Baltimore, without anyone challenging him." Blue could see his right hand man wheels spinning.

"So you telling me, you could make this happen?" Ricky asked, somewhat sold on the idea.

"For sure! I know his routine. Every Sunday at 2 p.m., he's at Cherry Hill Park, right off Cherryland Road and Reedbird Avenue, with four of his boys or bodyguards. I even know where his main bitch lives. She has a spot on Deacon Hill Court. I've been checking out this punk ass niggah for awhile. Our time is now!"

"We got to make a serious statement, because if we don't, we gonna have a lot of mutha-fuckas gunning for us from out of town; including the local police." Ricky replied, looking Blue in his eyes.

"Shit, after the statement we're going to make, we'll have the Mayor and the Police Commissioner on our payroll." Blue said with a smile, as he lit up a blunt.

"I hear that." Ricky laughed, as both men dapped.

"Check me one hour after the street lights come on, so we can make this happen." Blue informed, as he took a puff on the blunt, before passing it to Ricky.

*****

A week later, Blue, Ricky and their crew were ready to put their plan into effect. They were dressed in black and wearing ski mask, as five tinted black Denali's, rolled up Reedbird Avenue to observe the biggest dealer in Baltimore via New York. Blue dialed a number on his cell and the last Denali in their caravan pulled off and parked on the corner of Cherryland Avenue and Deacon Hill Court.

"Do you believe this shit?" Ricky blurted out, as the five men started walking toward the parked SUV's. Blue started laughing as if someone had just told a joke.

"These dumb niggah's must think we're the feds." Blue chimed in. Ricky opened the sunroof, as Maurice did the same in the SUV posted on Deacon Court. Ricky began to feel that something wasn't right, as he looked around.

Savannah

Why would they be walking toward us without fear? They don't know if we are assassins or the law. He kept thinking as his head turned from left to right. Blue was very ambitious, smart and cautious but he overlooked one thing, he underestimated his opponent. While Blue was doing surveillance on his rival, he was being checked out. When the SUV's pulled up on the block, they had already run the plates. They knew the men in the SUV's weren't the police; and although none of the tags led back to Blue or anyone in his crew. The dealer figured it was a robbery.

"Fuck! This is a set up." Ricky yelled, as people suddenly appeared from everywhere, with automatic weapons. A gunfight ensued between the intended target and the occupants in the four SUV's. The heavy bombardment of gunshots echoed throughout the community. Shots rang out from the vehicles as they scrambled trying to steer clear of certain death. It looked like a war scene from Iraq, except it was in the streets on the south side of Baltimore.

Hearing the gunfire, Maurice sped in the direction of where the sound was coming from. His crew made a u-turn, turning left onto Cherryland Road, heading towards Reedbird Avenue. Turning left again onto Reedbird. Maurice could see two SUV's heading toward Potee Street. The other two were bullet riddled with the occupants inside dead.

"What the fuck are they doing?" Maurice blurted out as both fleeing SUV's stopped. The one in the rear began burning rubber as it backed up about a hundred feet and suddenly stopped. Bluish white smoke filled the air from the spinning of the tires as Maurice pulled alongside the stopped SUV and laid heavy cover fire. A seventeen-year-old named Peewee exited the vehicle and snatched up a wounded gunman that was no older than fifteen and shoved him inside the vehicle. Bullets were still flying and the three remaining Denali's sped away crossing over Potee Street, before turning left onto South Hanover Street, heading toward I-95. Ricky and Maurice may have been young, but they were experienced like seasoned combat veterans; equal to the child soldiers of Africa.

Once out of harm's way, they pulled over in an industrial park, parking lot to assess the situation. Blue was shot in the abdomen and was bleeding badly.

"We need to get him to a hospital." Ricky said, in a concerned voice.

"Let's put him in my vehicle, mine ain't shot up like y'all's," Maurice spoke, walking back to bring the SUV around. Blue motioned for Maurice to stop. He wanted the three to hear what he had to say including the guys who stood guard watching the prisoner.

"Rick, this is your shit now. Make sure you get all my money. I need you to look out for my mom and sister. My mom isn't going to take any of this money, so just make sure all her bills are paid. Make sure you hit my sister up with some pocket change and put the rest in a college fund for her."

"Man, come on with that shit. I ain't got time for that. You gonna have to do that." Ricky replied, unsure of what else to say.

"We wasting time talking, let's go!" Peewee said impatiently.

Ricky stood there expressionless. Maurice immediately knew that Blue was dead from the expression on his brother's face. Ricky leaned over and closed Blue's eyes. He and Peewee removed his body from the vehicle and laid him out on the ground, as if he was in a casket; about fifteen yards away from the parked vehicles. Maurice walked to the vehicle and snatched their prisoner by the collar and handed him over to Ricky. Peewee opened the trunk area and retrieved an ax.

"Yo, you know the drill. You gonna tell us what we want to hear and need to know." Ricky informed their young prisoner. Seeing the ax in Peewee's hand, the young boy began spilling his guts. He told all he knew, what his mama knew, and what he thought the guy down the street knew, and what his dead father knew.

"You live with your mother?" Peewee asked.

"Yeah" He replied, visibly shaken.

"Well, your mama ain't gonna see your face again." The young boy eyes widened as Peewee swung the ax severing his head from his body. Blood flew everywhere as the headless body fell to the ground. It was business as usual, as far as Ricky and Maurice was concerned. Chopping off a head or two didn't faze them one bit.

Savannah

"Set these two ablaze." Ricky instructed Maurice, referring to the two bullet riddled Denali's. Ricky then walked over to the severed head, picked it up and tossed it into one of the burning vehicles. They gathered into the last remaining vehicle, undaunted by what had just occurred and sped off to finish the job.

"You know what; I'm drop you niggah's off. Me, Marcus and Peewee, are gonna finish what Blue and I set out to do. We'll be more effective with less."

A few hours later in the dark, undetected and standing on the north side of the kingpin's girlfriend's house, the three were about to complete the mission. Looking through the iron barred window, Ricky couldn't see anything, but he could hear someone having sex. Realizing there was no way to get inside, Ricky had to think quickly. He sent Maurice back to the SUV, to retrieve two red plastic ten gallon gas containers filled with gasoline, along with a small bucket. There was no sound or movement in the house when Maurice returned.

"They must be asleep," Maurice said, looking at his brother.

"Peewee, take one of the containers and go to the other side of the house and wait for me." Peewee did as he was told, and moved stealthily to a position on the other side of the house. Ricky filled the bucket half way with gasoline and threw the contents on the roof area and sides of the house, without making much noise. He repeated the same thing on the other side. He then took the remaining gasoline and made a trail leading away from the house. The three young assassins positioned themselves a safe distance, staying undetected and lit the gasoline trail leading to the house. Within a few seconds the house was engulfed in flames. The occupants in the house never had a chance escaping.

"If you don't remember anything else, remember this . . . A piece of pussy will get you hurt, if not killed, if you ain't on top of your business." Peewee said in a whisper. With the successful takedown of one of the most feared dealer now behind them; Ricky, Maurice, and Peewee became the youngest and most powerful drug dealers in Baltimore.

Their organization ruled the streets with fear and quality product along with intimidation and an unparallel viciousness and cruelty that were never seen before. Years' later and now grown men, Ricky, Maurice and Peewee's empire covered all of D.C. and most of Maryland. With the Mayor and Police Commissioner in their back pocket, they were now untouchable, or so they thought.

CHAPTER FOUR
"I hope not mama, I hope not"

Savannah was finally released after spending two months at Washington Hospital Center. But she had another six months of physical therapy, to get her close to her normal self. She had a broken right arm and left leg. She lost a kidney, had a damaged spleen and her uterus was beyond repair. The doctor's told her that she wouldn't be able to have any more children. God had blessed Savannah and her late husband with two beautiful boys and since Marcus was no longer here, she wasn't trying nor did she want any more children.

Savannah had put the house up for sale. It was no way she could continue to live in that house, with those awful memories. She and her two sons moved in with her parents in White Plains, Maryland for a little while. It gave her the support she needed to heal emotionally, while her body healed physically. The change of scenery diverted her sons' attention from the tragedy of their father's murder, while they enjoy precious time with their grandparents.

One early afternoon, on the way back home from one of her therapy sessions, her mother had to make a stop at the bank. Savannah decided to wait for her in the car. She sat there, watching people scurrying in and out of the financial institution; making deposits and withdrawals, her mind drifted and she began to think about Marcus. The more she thought about the man that had her heart, the more upset she became. Tears rolled down her cheeks, resting on her chin, before falling onto her shirt, as she began reminiscing about the great times they had. Thinking it would be like that until they were very old. Savannah could feel herself getting moist when she started thinking how he had control of her body with just a touch. More tears found their way from her eyes that made a road down her cheeks. Savannah thoughts were interrupted, when the front passenger door opened.

Savannah

"Are you okay baby?" Her mother spoke with concerned.

"I'm alright mama. I was just thinking about Marcus. It's hard mama, so damn hard." Savannah replied as she wiped her face, with the back of her hand.

"Honey, do you think the police are going to let these people get away with what they've done to you and Marcus?"

"I hope not mama, I hope not."

"It's going to be alright baby. Get yourself well for Devin and Chance. They really need you honey." Placing her hand on the right side of Savannah's face and gently massaging her cheek.

As days turned into weeks and weeks into months, Savannah could feel herself healing and getting stronger. After calling several times to the federal agents that questioned her at the hospital, to see where they were with the case, she was informed by them, that her case was turned over to the Charles County Sheriff's Department; since that's the county, where the crime had taken place.

She started getting upset with the run-around that she was receiving about her case and was getting short on patience. Savannah wanted to know why she and her husband were targeted, because they didn't do anything to anyone. She was very thankful, that her children weren't home at that time. After waiting in the lobby of the sheriff's department for what seemed like an eternity, she was informed by one of the detective's handling the case that the department was working diligently on finding someone; but so far they didn't have any new leads. She looked at the disheveled Caucasian detective, in his wrinkle white shirt, stained tie and worn shoes, like he must think she's a fool.

"How could you stand there and tell me that you are working diligently on the case, but have no new leads?" He didn't say anything; he just stood there looking at her. She became so disgusted, she turned and walked away.

"Mrs. Carrington! Mrs. Carrington!" The detective called out. Savannah ignored him as she continued walking toward the exit. When she got to the door an African American deputy was coming into the station. He looked her up and down, then paused for a split second at her southern region, and saw how her figure was working the new jeans she was wearing, before asking.

Brooklen Borne

"Can I help you ma'am?" He really had no interest in helping her. He only wanted to help himself to what was between my legs, with a meaningless introduction.

"Yes lover you can," She replied. A smile appeared on his face.

"You can help that detective standing there with that stupid look on his face; find some leads to who was behind my husband's murder." The smile on his face quickly disappeared, as Savannah continued through the double glass doors and toward her car. The only thing she was sure of, was that somebody was going to pay and she might have to administer justice herself, because she had no confidence in the police finding out anything. *My husband's death will not go unpunished,* she thought to herself as she drove through downtown La Plata; towards Waldorf.

*****

A few more months had passed when one of Savannah's cousins' in Baltimore gave her some information about a drug dealer named Maurice Fontayne from D. C. She told her Maurice was about to do some serious time, a life sentence without the possibility of parole at the Federal Correctional Institution in Cumberland County, Maryland. His brother Ricky, who is the major player in the DMV (D.C., Maryland and Virginia) drug business, was having no parts of that. He ordered a hit on the federal judge that was presiding over his younger brother's case. Ricky wanted to send a message, that his brother better not get serve any time, or else other political figures associated with his brothers case, were going to die. Her cousin also told her, instead of the hit men going to 3285 Elsa Place; they came to Savannah's house at 3285 Elsa Avenue, and altered her life forever. The word on the street was that Ricky didn't give a shit that the people he sent hit the wrong house. He just chalked it up as a lesson learned. After receiving that tidbit of information, Savannah didn't care how long it took, or how many people she had to go through to get to him.

Savannah

Ricky was going to learn a valuable lesson when she was finished with him.

"Thank you so much. I appreciate the info."

"I got you baby, we're family." Her cousin replied, before hanging up.

Lying across the bed with her eyes closed Savannah thought. *I'm going to give him and all who was involved, a life altering experience, just like they gave me. When you administer your own justice, public opinion and law enforcement, want to label you a vigilante. Yet it took my cousin beating bushes on the street to get me information I wanted in only a few months. Whereas, the federal agents and the sheriff's department couldn't get me the information I needed because they were dragging their feet. If certain people want to call me a vigilante, then so be it. Those who are so quick to judge, I wonder what they would do, if they were in my shoes? Would they lay down or would they become the label they have crowned me with?*

CHAPTER FIVE
"I know I will have to answer on judgment day"

Savannah was sitting at her dining room table talking to God. "The bible reads that revenge is yours, Lord. I know I will have to answer for my sins on judgment day, but as they say on the streets, these people must get got!" She was about to break one of the Ten Commandments, the sixth one to be exact…thou shall not murder. Her cousin Trina and two of her girlfriends, who visited her every day while she was laid up in the hospital, would have joined her on her quest, if she had asked them to; but she had to do this endeavor alone. Savannah couldn't bare anyone else she truly cared about getting hurt or killed on her behalf. Now on bent knees, still talking to God, "I guess I'm being a hypocrite, but I asked you to give me strength and to protect me, while I seek revenge for my husband's death…Amen."

*****

Savannahs' cousin Trina who lives in Baltimore, has major connections in the streets, and through some of those connections, supplied her with names of a few people that were involved in altering her life. Trina gave her the name and place to meet the man who started this cycle of violence. Savannah was about to meet her first kill in Kensington, Maryland at an Asian restaurant called P.F. Chang. This was the beginning of many that was going to die by her hands. He was a low down crooked, bald headed white cop; named Victor Rose.

He would sell out his own mother and put his daughter on the corner for the right price. Victor was the one who supplied the wrong address for the hit on the federal judge. That's why the police didn't have any leads, because one of their own was involved.

Savannah

And just because certain people have guns and badges, doesn't mean they are really out here to protect the public. They are only out to do a lot of injustice to some people. No matter what profession one is a part of, there is always someone in the organization that will screw it up for everyone else, and Victor is one of those screw ups.

He was sitting at the bar when Savannah walked in wearing a form-fitting blue silk dress with white accessories, four-inch blue leather pumps showcasing her sculptured calves with a white leather purse to match. She positioned herself a few seats down from him with her legs crossed over so he could see her thigh as her dress rose up a little. About a minute later she made eye contact with him and followed up on their connection with a smile that would have made a priest's penis harden. He sent Savannah a drink and she invited him over to sit with her. She gave him this fake story with tear-filled eyes about how she caught her man in bed with another woman and how it hurt her so bad. So, she was going to get revenge by meeting a handsome man and getting laid herself. That's all Victor needed to hear. He was a ready and willing partner to be the man she could use for revenge against her husband.

After a couple of more drinks over dinner Victor had secured a room at the Mandarin Oriental in south west D.C. No sooner than they entered the room, he began kissing Savannah while his hands explored her body. She was avoiding his tongue from going into her mouth, because he wasn't going to have that type of enjoyment. Not to mention she also had a razor blade stashed there. A trick, she remembered from her younger days; growing up in Detroit. The more she avoided his tongue, the more it seemed to get him excited, especially when he could see her nipples protruding through her silk dress. He pinned Savannah against the wall and started kissing her neck and he began grinding on her, as if he was a fifteen year old, getting to third base for the first time.

"I want to give you a show, before I throw this pussy on you." Savannah said in a seductive tone.

"Please do baby." Victor replied with a smile, as he held onto her hips; still grinding on her.

"Yeah baby. I want you to take off your clothes and lay on the bed." In no time Victor clothes were on the floor and he stood in his birthday suit with his little penis at the ready.

Savannah almost broke out in laughter, because she never saw a penis that small with a hard-on. As he lay down on the bed, she said to him. "I want you to stroke it, while I strip for you." He smiled and licked his lips, as he stroked himself. Savannah began taking off her clothes like an exotic dancer. A few minutes later, she was down to her black Victoria Secret see through bra and panties. He had snatched Savannah up and threw her down on the bed. The way he held onto her hips, she came right out her panties, almost swallowed the razor blade; that she had stashed in her mouth. He caught her off guard as he immediately began eating her out. She almost came in his mouth immediately. Savannah couldn't believe it. His mouth compensated for his small package.

"Wow baby, hold up!" Savannah blurted as she pushed down on the top of his head, to get him off the pussy. Her vagina was trying to get a mind of its own, since it hasn't had that type of attention in a very long time. Somehow she regained her composure and took control once again.

"I can eat you out until you fall unconscious," Victor replied seductively licking his lips.

"I have no doubt in that, but this is my show." She walked over to her purse and retrieved a small rolled up piece of duct tape and seductively wined her hips as she unraveled the tape. Before placing it over his mouth, she told him. "The fuckin', I'm about to put on you, I'm gonna have you screaming my name the second you're inside me." After placing the piece of tape over his mouth, she took off her bra, revealing her firm 34D's. Victor under size penis twitched when he saw her mouth watering breast. His throbbing member pressed against her canal entrance, when she straddled him. Savannah never killed a person before and she was nervous and scared, but she put her mind somewhere else for what she was about to do. She started kissing his chest, as he placed his hand on the side of her face. As Savannah came to the side of his belly button, she pulled the razor blade from her mouth without him noticing. In one quick motion, she took a hold of his penis and

Savannah

sliced the vein. He started to scream but his scream was muffled by the tape on his mouth. He put both hands on his severed member. Savannah then bought the razor across his jugular. He had one hand on his groan area and the other on his neck. A few minutes later his body lay motionless on the bed. The once white 450 count sheets were now red with his blood. She paused for a minute to stare at his lifeless body, before cleaning herself up and leaving the room.

Savannah still felt nervous, but relieved as she walked away from the hotel to her car located a block away. Once at the car, she sat behind the wheel with her eyes closed, to give herself a minute before driving off; hoping she had covered all her tracks. She knew how cops can get when one of their own is killed. They will stop at nothing to find out who did it, and when that person is found, they may not make it to lockdown.

*****

Thanks to the information Trina was supplying Savannah with; she had almost everyone that was involved in the botched hit, set up for their death date. Savannah was surprised as how little effort it took to touch, the so called untouchables. Most men are creatures of habit, show them some cleavage and leg, with a dress that shows off your assets and they are hooked. Her mission was far from over. Her goal was to take out the man behind this nightmare, Ricky Fontayne a.k.a. Pretty Ricky "the" drug kingpin of the DMV. Savannah was thinking he probably looks like death, four times over and gave himself that name to boost his ego. Once she have located him and find out his routine, she will seduce him, reel him in and end his life. A few days later, her other cousin Shanna, Trina's younger sister had hooked her up with a photo of Pretty Ricky; that she had obtained from one of his recent ex-girlfriend.

Savannah and Shanna served together in the same unit when they were in the Air Force. Shanna wouldn't have a problem taking Ricky out herself, if her cousin asked her to. She told Savannah Ricky would be coming to DC to hang out at a club in a couple of weeks. Savannah was wrong about Ricky she thought to herself as she pulled his picture from the envelope; he's a handsome brown-skinned brother in his early thirties. His hair cut low, well-groomed with strong features and dresses very nice. He looks about six-two and well built. If this photo does him justice like this, he must really be something in person. *It's a shame I have to kill him.*

*****

The ringing phone jarred Savannah from her peaceful sleep. With her eyes barely opened she looked at the caller ID and saw it was Shanna.

"Hello."

"Savannah, wake up girl. This is Shanna; Trina told me to remind you."

Stretching and yawning, "Hey Shanna, what's up? Remind me of what?"

"Your boy is going to be down your way tonight."

"What boy?"

"Pretty Ricky! You need to wake your ass up, so I know you got this information, I'm about to pass on."

"I'm up. I'm up. Damn girl," Savannah replied, still trying to gather herself. "He's going to be at H2O tonight. So make sure you make contact with him. This may be your one and only chance to get this close to him."

"Is he going to be there for sure?"

"Without a doubt baby girl, he's going to be there. My friend Abdul who owns the club told me he was shutting down a section for a private party for a dude called Ricky Fontayne. He told me, Ricky is known for spending a lot of many in the clubs. Girl, talking about clubs, the food there is off the chain; I've eaten there before."

"Stay focused Shanna." Savannah told her; now fully awake.

"Any way I wanted to give you that bit of info before I head out of town."

"Where are you going?"

"My man is taking me to Vegas for the weekend."

"That sounds nice."

Savannah

"It's going to be more than nice. I'm gonna try to break his back." She replied back with a chuckle.

"You mean break his bank?"

"No, I mean break his back. I'm gonna ride that long snake, like never before."

"See nasty one, that's too much information." They both laughed.

"If I wasn't going away this weekend, I would be there with you for back up."

"I know you would. Thanks sweetie for the heads up."

"Not a problem."

"Talk to you later and be safe in Vegas."

"Okay, I will. Tell the boys I said hi."

"For sure!"

" Bye."

"Bye."

*****

Later that night, Savannah went to the club to introduce herself to the dead man, who brought her to the world; she never wanted to come to. She wore a look at this body, don't you want to fuck me red dress which revealed her Beyonce legs and Nicki Minaj booty. Her cousin Michael, acting as her chauffeur opened the door, all eyes were on her, as she stepped from the smoke-grey Maybach. Her intended victim was standing outside, not far from the club entrance; with another guy, as she walked with a sexy swagger towards the entrance. She had their full attention. Taken aback by this beautiful woman walking towards him, he knew he had to have her. He opened the door for her and with a smile spoke.

"Good evening pretty lady."

"Good evening." She responded with a smile.

"My name is Ricky; Ricky Fontayne."

"Shauntay Justice is mine." Not giving him her real name.

"I like your pretty light brown eyes."

"They are the real thing and not contacts. In case you were wondering."

"No sexy, I can tell that's the real color of your eyes. Well Shauntay, I hope to have a dance with you, before the night ends."

"We'll see," she replied while still smiling, as she continued into the club. Taking a seat at the bar, she ordered an Apple Martini; it wasn't long before Ricky came and sat next to her. They ended up having a few more drinks. They danced a little and talked about nothing she was really interested in, but had to fake it like she was for the sake of what she was going to do to him. He was acting like a perfect gentleman; saying and doing all the right things, but she knew his game. If she was one of those stupid bitches, he would have had her hook, line and sinker with her on her back and legs in the "V" position. If only he knew she was setting him up, to end his miserable life. It was three in the morning and Savannah was ready to leave, but not without putting the finishing touches on Ricky.

"Would you mind walking me to my car?"

"Not at all pretty lady."

"Ricky, I noticed throughout the evening this gentleman following your every move."

"Yeah, that's my bodyguard; Bruce."

"So I'm in the company of a very important person."

"You can say that."

"Well, it's been a pleasure to meet you, very important person, with a bodyguard." He chuckled.

"The pleasure was all mine. Are you doing anything later today when you wake up?" He asked with an eagerness to be in her presence. She pulled out her blackberry and started pushing numbers, as if she was really checking her schedule.

"I'm free. I have nothing scheduled."

"Sounds like a winner then. I promise not to keep you up late."

"Good. I wouldn't want you to have any problems at work, come Monday."

"That won't be a problem. I'm the boss." He replied with a grin, as he handed her a card with his address and phone number on it. 36-38 South Paca Street, Baltimore.

"Near East Pratt Street," Savannah said, looking back at him.

"I'm impressed."

Savannah

"I went to a lot of concerts up there. I know the area well." She said, placing the card in her purse.

"Where do you live gorgeous?" Savannah just looked him with no expression. "Hmm a mystery woman, okay. Where ever your home may be, have a safe trip there."

"Thank you." She replied, catching him sneaking a glimpse at her luscious legs, as he closed the door. Savannah thought to herself, she had a little too much to drink, because she was horny and sleepy. She needed to get home, take a cold shower and get to bed.

"Michael, get me out of here."

"I got you cuz. Sit back and relax." Savannah lowered the window a little, to get some air as he started the car. Closing her eyes, she sank in the comfortable position.

"How in the hell did Rickey get in this car?" Savannah thought. He grabbed her behind the head, pulling her toward him and started kissing her. Their tongues met and the kiss was so satisfying and intense, she instantly became wet. He laid her down gently and lowered her panties and inserted two fingers into her eagerly awaiting for something to be inside her, pussy. Her back arched with every movement of his finger. His soft mouth felt beautifully warm on her breast as he sucked and licked on her nipples. Their kiss became more intense, as he pulled out his sugar cane and slid it inside her. "Oh shit, I'm about to cum all over his sweet dick." Savannah couldn't believe she was giving up the goodies, to the man who was behind the killing of her husband, but it was feeling too good to stop.

"Savannah, wake up! We're here." Michael informed, as he shook her. She had dozed off shortly after they drove away from the club. She couldn't believe she was dreaming about Ricky. Those drinks she had at the club, put her in a state she didn't like....not in control.

"What the hell were you dreaming about girl? You were moaning and shit. Is everything alright with you?"

"Yeah, I'm good. I just had a crazy dream."

"Sound like you was fuckin' somebody."

"Shut up with your crazy ass." Savannah replied feeling a little embarrassed. Little did he know, he was on point, but she wouldn't ever let him on that he was right. He dropped her off in front of a hotel in DC, after circling the monuments a couple of times, making sure they weren't being followed. Although she didn't want anyone with her during these trying and dangerous times, Michael was the only family she allowed to be with her, because he's a martial arts expert and former Marine.

"Are you okay to drive home?" Michael asked with raised eyebrows.

"I'm good. That short nap helped me out."

"Alright, I'll pick you up tomorrow cuz. You know, I'm not letting you go to B-more, by yourself."

"Thank you baby, I appreciate you looking out for me."

"Marcus was my man. Plus your mom…Aunt Inez would put her foot in my butt if she thought I knew what was going on and let you do this by yourself. So anything that needs to be done to make it right with you, I'm down. No matter what it is, you feel me?"

"I feel you."

"I'll see you tomorrow around four. Savannah, make sure you tell Aunt Inez, I said hi."

"I will." She ensured, as she exited the Maybach and walked through the doors of the hotel lobby. Michael pulled away as she entered the elevator. She exited on the P3 level of the parking lot, where she was parked and got in her car and drove home making sure that she was still not being followed. Savannah got on the 395 ramp and twenty-five minutes later she arrived at her parent's house. Every one was asleep, except for her father. He waited up for her just like he use to when she was a teenager.

"Hey daddy, I know you not waiting up for me?" Savannah asked kissing him on the cheek.

"Why not baby girl, this wouldn't be the first. You want something to eat?"

"No daddy, I'm good. I had a bite while I was out."

"Come here baby girl. Have a seat I want to talk to you." She followed her father into the kitchen, and sat down at the table.

Savannah

"I haven't said anything to your mother, but I know what you've been up to."

"You do?" Her heart skipped a beat, as she replied. "Why didn't you tell mom?"

"To have her lose her mind and listen to her lecture the both of us, from sun up to sun down. No thank you." He chuckled.

"Dad..." He interrupted her before she could finish her sentence.

"I'm confident that you know what you're doing. If anything were to happen to your mother or my grand children, like what happened to Marcus, I would be out there doing the same thing honey. But I'm going to worry about you until the day I die. Baby, remember this, only eliminate the threat. No unnecessary killing. I hope getting Ricky will be the end of this all and begin the healing process." Her father paused for a minute, before asking. When she was going after Ricky? With her mouth now wide open, she couldn't respond. She couldn't believe her father knew so much.

"Baby, I'm waiting for an answer."

"Tomorrow! In twenty-four hours it will be done."

"I hope when you're finish with Ricky Fontayne everyone that helped you, will keep their mouth shut. I don't want anything leading back to our family."

"I have a loyal crew daddy."

"Be safe honey. I don't want me or your mother trying to explain to our grand babies that something real bad happened to their mother, you understand?" He said as he held her hand, looking into her eyes.

"Michael is coming with me."

"I know that too." He replied as they both broke out in laughter.

"Go kiss your babies, and get some sleep." Savannah turned to walk away, then stopped in her tracks and turned around.

"Daddy, how do you know so much?"

"Let's just say, your mother and I former place of employment, keeps us in-the-know business. Go kiss your babies honey."

CHAPTER SIX
"Damn baby, what a beautiful picture"

Savannah and Michael arrived at Ricky's place at five o'clock. His loft was located in downtown Baltimore near the harbor. It looked like something a movie star would live in. They parked down the block, out the sight of the security cameras mounted outside on various areas of the building.

"I don't feel good about staying in the car." Michael said as he turned around to look at her.

"I'll be alright. Just take care of the video feed."

"You're sure about this?" He asked with a concerned expression.

"I'm sure Michael. I can handle this."

"If any thing goes wrong, make sure you hit me up on the cell. You do have my number on speed dial? Don't you?"

"You know I do."

Savannah stepped out the car, and walked toward the building, fixing her skirt. A few seconds after ringing the bell, Ricky opened the door with a smile. He looked at her as he stuck his head out the door and took a glance left and right, to make sure he wasn't under surveillance.

"Hello beautiful." Ricky said, as he greeted Savannah with a kiss on the cheek.

"Hello handsome."

"Please come inside." He took a hold of her hand, assisting her inside, as take a glimpse of her derriere.

His loft was decorated exquisitely. The walls were of exposed brick with original wood beams and floors. The open layout had high ceilings with large windows that gave a view overlooking the harbor, was just spectacular. As they walked further into the loft, Savannah saw this guy playing with a play station on

Savannah

what look like a sixty inch plasma. The closer she got to him; she noticed it was his body guard, Bruce.

"Hey lady, how are you doing?" He spoke without taking his eyes off the screen.

"I'm fine."

"Good! Good!" He responded. She quickly turned her attention back to Ricky, when he asked her did she want a drink; while he gave her the nickel tour.

"Sure, that would be nice." He fixed both of them a glass of champagne. Savannah hadn't had champagne since that awful night when she and Marcus were shot. They continued to tour this beautiful work of art, which was turned into a home. The last room he showed her was the master suite. It was something right out of Life Styles of the Rich and Famous. It was located on the second mezzanine level overlooking the floor below. Savannah loved the open floor plan. The place was carpeted from wall to wall in a plush snow white. At the far end of the room, and the focal point, rested his king size bed that you had to go up two steps to reach. The comforter was white with black speckles. Behind the bed was a huge fire place, flanked by mirrors on each side of it. On the opposite end of the bed was a breath taking view of the Baltimore skyline. This loft was put together with much thought.

"Since we're up here, let's get undressed, and get in the Jacuzzi."

"I didn't bring a bathing suit." Savannah replied with a seductive under tone.

"I have something for you to slip into." Ricky went into the bedroom and appeared a short time later wearing blue swim trunks.

"Try this on." He said with a smile, while handing her a tee shirt that came midway up her thighs. This was her introduction to turn up the heat. Ricky had refilled their glasses, and then he posted up in the Jacuzzi. She slowly disrobe and bent over at the waist to pick up the Tee shirt from the floor giving him a back view of her firm booty and shaved vagina. Savannah knew she was going to have to sleep with him, if her plan was going to work. The technique she used on the cop and others will not work in this case. Ricky wasn't going to take his pants off unless he's was going to be inside her. This may be her only chance to take him out. Security is low, they are not in public, so there will be no witnesses, this is a now or never moment. She said a quick prayer and asked her late husband to forgive her, for what she was about to do.

"Damn baby, what a beautiful picture." Ricky said, while taking a sip from his glass. "Pretty lady, how did you get those scars on that perfect figure of yours?" At this point Savannah had snuggled up against him with her glass of champagne.

"Two assholes did a number on me. I really don't want to go into now."

"I hope you returned the favor." Looking into his eyes, without blinking, she responded.

"No! But I took care of most of them already. It's one more knuckle head I have to deal with." Then she took a sip of champagne.

"Do you need help?"

"No!" She replied, but what she really wanted to say, it's your ass I'm talking about dealing with stupid.

She turned around and leaned up against him. Laying her head back onto his shoulder, she felt him get an instant hard on. He started massaging her breast as she slowly moved her ass up and down against his pole. One of his hands departed from her firm breast and traveled south to spend time playground. It must have been the champagne that was making her feel relaxed and putting her in the horny mode. She turned around and their tongues began to play tag with one another. Savannah broke away and kissed him on his lips and said, "I think we should move this to the bedroom."

"I agree." Ricky responded as they stepped out the Jacuzzi and removed their wet clothes. They let what little they had on, fall to the floor were they stood. The glass of champagne had her going. She couldn't take her eyes off his penis it was long and curved slightly to the left. Even though the sight made her salivate, she had to stay focus. He took a plush towel and wrapped it around her before picking her up to carrying her towards the bed. While walking to the bedroom, he whispered in her ear, "I wanted you the moment you stepped out that Maybach, at the club." She just smiled

Savannah

and rubbed the back of his head. Gently laying her down on the bed, he gave her a soft kiss on the lips before departing for the bathroom. Savannah's Coach Purse was on the floor beside the bed. She reached inside for her trusty straight razor and placed it underneath the pillow. A few seconds later Ricky emerged with a rubber on his soldier.

"Wow!" She said with a seductive tone, as she parted her legs. He went down on her and started eating her out. Her toes began to curl like a bird holding onto a branch. Savannah soft moans became louder and within minutes, he had her screaming, like she was being killed. Bruce came running up the stairs and into the bedroom, her nakedness on display. Savannah's face was flushed and her body was still trembling from the intense orgasm that ran through her body. Ricky looked at Bruce as if to say get the fuck out the room. Bruce smiled while throwing his hands in the air as he walked away.

It was no more than five minutes, and Ricky had Savannah flowing like Niagara Falls. Her orgasms were so intense, she couldn't stop shivering. Her breathing was very heavy and her eyes were rolled up so far in her head, she could see her brain. Ricky paused long enough to savor the sight of his effects on her. He told her to turn over, and grabbed her by the hips and with her head down and ass up, began tossing her salad, while vigorously massaging her clit, with his index finger. Savannah was moaning uncontrollably with every lick of his tongue. Ricky worked her like that for about thirty minutes, and she began squirting. He then brought her to the edge of the bed and put his erect penis inside her and instantly she started to have multiple orgasms as if she was having convolutions. The way he was putting the dick to her, Savannah began to have flashbacks of her husband. She called out Marcus's name a few times, while her face was buried in the pillow. Ricky probably didn't understand what she was saying anyway. All he cared about was having his way with her. An hour and countless positions later, he finally came. Savannah screamed out God name three times, as she climaxed with him.

As she was trying to control her erratic breathing, he pulled off the condom and stuck his penis in her mouth. Savannah began sucking it instinctively, before she caught herself and gently pushed him away. For just a moment, a wave of guilt came over her for giving this murderer of her husband the joy of her body; but she had a personal vendetta to score and she was going to get the job done by any which way she could.

"Damn! I haven't been worked like that in a long time."

"I wanted to be deep inside you the second I saw you baby." He responded with his eyes still closed. This was Savannah's do-or-die moment to take him out. She started kissing and nibbling on his ear while talking dirty and stroking him. Ricky's pole was back at full erection as she stoked it firmly. She leaned over and started licking up the shaft as she continued a steady stroke, getting closer to the head of his penis, while sliding her right hand underneath the pillow. She opened her mouth as if she was going to give him a serious blowjob. Her lips were just about to touch the tip of his penis, when she brought her hand from underneath the pillow and severed his dick from the base. Blood spewed everywhere, including on her. She jumped out the bed and ran into the bathroom holding a handful of flesh and flushed it down the toilet.

"You'll be a dick-less son-of-a-bitch until the day you die, mutha-fucka." She spat in a whispered to him as she walked from the bathroom wiping blood from her face and hands; with one of his towels.

"Oh God! Oh God!" Ricky kept screaming out. He couldn't say anything else as a pool of blood formed around his waist and thighs; while he rolled around in the bed. Bruce never came back up stairs. He probably thought Ricky was having a major orgasm and didn't want to interrupt him; in fear of what Ricky might do to him, if he did. Savannah continued to wipe blood off of her while still holding onto the razor; she put her dress and heels on and quickly walked out the room, then down the stairs.

"What the fuck?" Bruce blurted out, as he looked at Savannah holding the straight razor. He hastily walked toward her and when he got close enough, she came across his neck slicing his jugular. Bruce grabbed his neck with both hands as he fell to his knees. Blood was gushing from his neck, like a Saudi oil well. He

Savannah

fell forward onto his face dead, as blood began to cover the wooden floor beneath him.

Ricky staggered down the stairs with both hands on his groin, screaming obscenities at Savannah. Blood was still gushing down his legs. Savannah grabbed a statue of a Greek figure from the coffee table, walked over to him and hit him upside the head; knocking him out. She then wiped her prints from the statue and placed the razor in Ricky's hand. She quickly cleaned herself off with baby wipes that she had brought with her, and placed each one she used in a plastic bag to take with her. Savannah wasn't going to leave any DNA behind. She looked in the floor length mirror quickly giving herself a look over before hastily leaving the house; grabbing Bruce's cell phone off the table on the way out. Closing the door with a handkerchief, Savannah casually walked back to the limousine.

"Mike, let's get the hell out of here." She then called 9-1-1 on Bruce's cell to inform them that she heard a lot of yelling and someone screaming for the police. Michael was looking at her through the rear view mirror all the time she was on the phone. Savannah gave the dispatcher the address then began disassembling the cell and throwing the pieces out the window, as they drove down the street.

"Are you good?" Michael asked, glancing at her through the rearview mirror while he kept his eyes on the road.

"I'm good, keep driving." Just as they turned the corner, they heard the police sirens in the distance. "You took care of the video feed?"

"Yeah, they won't have any recordings of you ever coming or going."

"Cool!"

*****

Savannah's handy work was featured on the late evening news. Bruce was dead but Ricky was still alive. The media made the incident seem like it was a drug deal gone wrong. They also found eight kilos of cocaine and two hundred and fifty thousand dollars in large bills in the freezer. Mr. Pretty Ricky will be going away for a very long time with his record. Savannah smiled as she thought Ricky won't be seeing the light of day again. She set out to kill all those involved in her husband's murder and she succeeded in her endeavors. The media continued to say, the police believe it was a rival drug organization from New York that Ricky's been feuding with, and trying to move in of territory ran by Ricky Fontayne. When in actuality, it was Savannah, who did the damage. There was no need to go any further with her killing spree. Ricky was the person who started all this mayhem and he was getting his just deserve. She could begin to heal emotionally and start to live once more. Her children needed her and now she can give them the attention they desperately wanted and needed.

    Some people might say that she was a vigilante, or judge her for issuing her brand of street justice. But do you really know how you're going to react when something tragic happens in your life, especially when it wasn't your fault? She didn't get pleasure in hurting people nor did she like taking lives. She was a law-abiding citizen who paid her taxes and so forth, like everyone else. But when her husband was murdered and her body riddled with bullets, almost leaving her children as orphans, well, like any true wife or mother, she had to do what she had to do. The police didn't have any suspects in her case and they didn't seem to be hard at work, trying to get anyone; maybe due to one of their own was involved. Waiting on answers from various law enforcement agencies to do something, look what happened. She ended up solving her own homicide case.

    Savannah made some calls and had some bushes shook and staying two steps ahead of the police, she fulfilled what she had to do. Her father never did tell her how he knew what she was doing, but as long as he had her back, it didn't matter. She's just a woman that was in love with her husband, a husband that meant everything to her and their two boys.

    With the money she made from the sale of her home and the money from Marcus's insurance policy; Savannah was sitting well. She moved to North Carolina with her children, because there were too many painful memories in Maryland. At least with a new start in

Savannah

the Carolina's her sons and she could try to resume a normal life. She was afraid of a couple of things. Ricky may find out her real name and have some people come after her and her sons or do something to her mother and father. Savannah knew she couldn't let those thoughts consume her, because if Ricky decides to continue to be a thorn in her life, she will make sure to end his life.

CHAPTER SEVEN
"Without the possibility of parole"

     Savannah had a college friend named Andrew Johnson, which happened to work at the prison, where Ricky was doing his time. Andrew called her after her cousin Trina had contacted him and told him the story on what had happen, between the two. Savannah had confirmed Trina's story with Andrew, but didn't really want to get into details; not trusting him fully. She had moved out the state and on with her life and wanted to put that chapter behind her. Andrew told her; due to his position he listens to some inmates' phone conversations, due to their reputation of sending coded messages, to conduct illegal activities on the outside. One particular call Ricky made, had brought up a red flag he believed Savannah should know about; when he heard the name Shauntay Justice. The alias she used when she met Ricky. Andrew went on to tell her, Ricky was talking to some guy on the phone and supposedly had said. *"What the fuck had he ever done to Shauntay Justice? I treated her with respect, and then all of a sudden she flipped the script on a brother and cut my shit off. One way or another, I'm going to find a way to get that bitch back. I can't believe that bitch did this to me. Now I'm doing twenty-five to life without the possibility of parole, in this fuckin' place."*
     She thanked Andrew and asked, what were Ricky chances of escaping from there? He informed her, she had nothing to worry about because; no one has ever escaped from that prison. This is the place where the federal government sends its worst–of-the-worst prisoners; people who have murdered someone in or out of prison. It's nicknamed The Alcatraz of the Rockies, because it's home to some of the nation's most notorious criminals. He also assured her. "If you make it here, the odds are you'll be an old man when you get out…that is if you get out.

Savannah

If your behavior is not accordingly, you could serve your entire sentence in isolation. It's worst than being in Pelican Bay." That's another notorious prison in California. Savannah told Andrew thank you for the information and appreciated him looking out for her. Before hanging up, he told her he was going to send her a disk, of the conversation Ricky had with a visitor, about a week ago. He thought it might be important information for her to use at a later date.

After hanging up with Andrew, she got on the internet, to see what this prison was really about. The inmates there range from drug kingpins to international terrorists. Richard Reid the al-Qeada shoe bomber. Ramzi Yousef the mastermind behind the 1993 World Trade bombings. Eyad Ismoil, is serving over 200 years for driving the rental van holding the bomb in the World Trade Center attack. Yu Kikumura, Japanese Red Army terrorist is serving a thirty year bid, for transporting bombs in preparation for an attack on a military recruiting station. There are home grown terrorist here too. Timothy McVeigh, the Oklahoma City bomber, spent time there before getting transfer to Indiana, where his life was taken by the state. His partner Terry Nichols, is there doing life. The Unabomber, Theodore Kaczynski, is also there serving four life sentences.

Savannah received the disk a couple of days later. When she put the kids to bed, she poured a glass of White Merlot and put the disk in the computer and placed the headphones over her ears. The conversation went like this:

"Hey daddy, how are you doing?"
"I'm doing alright baby."
"Hello Karyn. You look great!"
"Thank you. How are you holding up?"
"I'm surviving. So tell me, why aren't you married?"
"Because (pause) I haven't met the right man yet."
"Yeah, right! You know you're still in love with me."
"Is that right?"
"That's right."

Brooklen Borne

"I'm not going to get into with you Ricky, in front of your daughter. (Silence) Peewee is also here to see you. I saw him pulling up in the parking lot as we were walking away from the car."

"Good, good. My little girl is all grown up and looking beautiful as ever. I'm very proud of you honey."

"Thank you daddy."

"I placed a thousand in your commissary account."

"Good looking out baby. I appreciate that."

"I still love you Ricky and I will make sure, you will want for nothing. (Silence) We have to leave. It's a long drive to the airport. We're flying back today. We'll try to visit next month."

"It was great seeing you Karyn. Thank you for bringing my daughter."

"Bye, baby girl."

"Bye daddy. I love you."

"I love you too."

Savannah later found out through her cousin Trina, that Karyn is Ricky's ex-wife and the step mother of his eighteen year old daughter. She didn't understand, how a family man, would have so much disregard for an innocent family well being. Then it hit her…what drug dealer would care.

CHAPTER EIGHT
"You have the right to remain silent"

When Savannah heard the door bell ring, it seemed like it took her forever to reach the door. She asked who it, as she looked through the peephole.

"Police, ma'am," was the response. Standing in front of her, were two police officers, one white and the other black.

"Are you Ms. Savannah Carrington?" One of the officers asked.

"Yes!"

"Ma'am, we have a felony warrant for your arrest. He began reading her, her rights.

"What is this all about?" Savannah asked, as the officer turned her around and placed her in handcuffs.

"Ma'am, do you understand the rights I have just read to you?"

"Yeah, but I would like to know, what is this all about?" Her heart was racing a mile a minute. Fear had set in her body, with the thought of her freedom being taken away.

"You're being charged for murder ma'am." Savannah legs almost gave out from beneath her as she tried to compose herself.

"Who in the hell have I supposedly had murdered?" They never answered her as they escorted her to the patrol car. "I need to call my lawyer. I'm not saying a word without a lawyer. As they drove away towards the station, one of the officers turned around and said.

"We don't like mutha-fuckas going around killing cops, like it's alright." Savannah just looked at him in shock. His partner who was staring at her through the rearview mirror injected.

Savannah

"Do you remember killing a detective by the name of Victor Clark at the Mandarin Oriental Hotel in D.C.? She just looked at him. Not saying a word, she was thinking, *Oh shit! How in the hell did they figure it was me? I left no prints, I wore a wig and no one in a million years would have recognized me.* Savannah couldn't believe it, from all the people she took out, she would get pinched for her first hit. They pulled into a vacant lot in a desolate part of town, behind a vacant building. The officer driving got out and opened her side of the door. He then positioned Savannah legs outside, while she stayed seated inside the cruiser. He gave her the meanest look, she ever saw on a person face, and then said half-aloud. "Since you like to fuck and kill police officers, we're gonna fuck the shit outta you, before taking you to the station."

The black officer held her legs, while the white one raised her skirt and pulled her panties down. Savannah kicked at him and she caught him on the chin with the heel of her shoe at full force. He stepped back for a second to recover from the shock of being kicked on the chin. The officer reared back and with a closed fist punched her in the jaw. Not only did she feel like he broke her jaw, but it also felt like her face had left the skull it was shaped around. Savannah fell backward in the horizontal position; hitting her head on the hard plastic seat. They both proceeded to unzipped their pants and put on condoms.

The black officer parted her legs and blurted. "We're gonna tear this pussy up." His partner then added. "Bitch, when we're done with your pussy, we're gonna fuck you in the ass." Savannah began to scream for help. She kicked and squirmed to gain her freedom, but it was useless. Her hands were still cuffed behind her back and the officer's were too strong. When one of the officers stuck his erect penis in her dry vagina, pain shot throughout her body; as if she was getting a tooth pulled without any Novocain.
"Ahhh!" Savannah screamed out, as she sat up in the bed in a cold sweat, looking from side to side and disorientated. She glanced over at the clock. It was four in the morning. Thank God it was only a dream, she thought. Savannah laid her head back down on the pillow for a minute to get herself. She didn't want to go back to sleep after that nightmare. She got out the bed and took a shower.

Brooklen Borne

*****

It's been three years since Savannah made the transition to North Carolina. She bought a beautiful three-bedroom ranch style home in Scotts County. The home is located in a golf community called Deercroft. The winters there are milder than up north, but the summers there, can be hot as hell. Overall, this is a beautiful place to raise a family or live out ones retirement years. Everything has been going well for Savannah and her sons, thus far. She had a nice job on Pope Air Force Base. Her children were doing well in school. They both finished the school year with honors. Life in North Carolina would have been perfect for her, if her husband was still with them. She was blessed to have a great support system. Her parents along with Marcus's parents have been a great help.

She and the kids were leaving for Maryland around midnight, so she could drop them off to spend the summer with both sets of grandparents. Savannah thanked God everyday for her boys; they have kept her going, through this ordeal. They also kept her alive because if she didn't have them, when she found out Marcus was murdered, she may have committed suicide.

CHAPTER NINE
"Tell me how it really went down"

While Savannah was packing Devin and Chance's clothes, to go to Maryland, she received another call from Andrew. He had told her, that he was sending her an overnight package with the conversation between Ricky and Peewee. He informed her, that she needed to be ready because they were coming after her. She asked who was coming for her, thinking it was the police. He told her some guy named Peewee, one of Ricky's friends. Her heart almost stopped.

"Do they know where I live?"
"I would say no, not from the phone transcripts."
"Alright, thanks Andrew for the heads up."
"You're welcome. If someone was coming after me or even thinking about it, I would hope someone give me heads up. Just watch yourself."
"I will! Thanks again Andrew. Bye-bye."

*****

Peewee is a slim brown skinned bald head brother; around five-nine, a hundred-sixty pounds. His reputation is worse than the character Omar on "The Wire." When he comes around, people scatter, because he is known for taking joy in dismembering people that crosses him or his friends.

"Ricky, what's going on brother?"
"What's up Peewee?" The two men dapped one another, with an embrace.
"I heard what the media was saying on how you ended up here. But I know the media is full of shit. They will sensationalize road kill if it would bring ratings."

Savannah

"You're right about that."

"Tell me how it really went down. Even though we are in the business we are in, we're never supposed to be having a conversation in a place like this."

"I had met this female named Shauntay Justice at club H2O in DC. We were feeling one another, so we decided to hook up the next day. She came over to my place around five in the evening; we had some drinks and chilled in the Jacuzzi, before moving the party to the bed, where we were going at it for about two hours. We were resting from a round of sex, then she started stroking my shit and was about to give me some head. Then all of a sudden she pulled out a straight razor from underneath the pillow and cut my shit off. Then she went into the bathroom and flushed it down the toilet, before going down stairs and slitting Bruce's throat. I staggered out the room holding the area, where my dick use to be, bleeding like crazy and she hit me on the head with a statue; knocking me out. When I came to, the police and E.M.S. were there, and I was holding a straight razor. That bitch planted it in my hand. Just like the way the fuckin' police do. How in the hell, will I be able to slit someone throat with my dick cut off? Now I'm pissing in a fuckin' bag."

"I feel for you."

"My lawyer has filed an appeal. He said it's a good chance, we will win the appeal. The new Mayor wanted to make a name for himself, by cleaning up Baltimore, so he wanted to use me for an example; instead of the true facts. If they want to cage someone, no matter what the evidence say, they are going to cage someone."

"You're right about that. It took me a minute to come visit you, because I was out the country when all this went down. The second I got back in town, I was filled in on what happened. So I jumped on the first smoking, to come and visit you."

"I understand. I knew you were out the country handling your business. So did the venture, worked out the way you wanted it to?"

"It worked out better than I anticipated. All your affairs will be taken care of." That was the signal for them to start talking in code.

"Do you remember spending all that time trying to get into Shauntay pants and after we drank all that liquor, she said she wasn't feeling you, because you pinched her nipple too hard?" Both men laughed. "But for some strange reason her girl friend Savannah Carrington was infatuated with you. (Her real name is Savannah Carrington). I couldn't believe she let you finger her, in front of everybody. (You were set up by her) She was pissed with you, when you went to pick her up and went to the wrong house, and the chic that opened the door started flirting with you. So you end up fucking her. (Her house was the one that was hit, instead of the judges' house.)

"Yeah man." Both men chuckled.

"Well the word is, her man heard about you getting the ass and he got pissed and left the bitch, after breaking her nose. (Her husband was killed that night.)

"How does her nose look?"

"It's fixed and she looks hot!

"Let her know, I want to come visit me." (I want her dead.)

"I'm a step ahead of you. I've already passed that info on to her." (I'm checking on her whereabouts as we speak.)

"Make sure you tell Savannah, to put three hundred on my commissary when she comes to visit." (I'll pay three hundred thousand, for any enforcer that kills her.)

"Not a problem."

"I miss sucking on those big tits." (Cut off her breast, before killing her.)

"I know that's right."

"What do her parents think about her hooking up with someone on lock down?" (Find her parents and you'll find her.)

"From my understanding, they don't care what she does or who she does it with." (They'll be easy to find.)

"That's good. Do me a favor, get my daughter a present; her birthday is coming up." (If she has any kids, kill them too.)

"Don't let it be two months before you visit again. (I want her dead within sixty days.)

Savannah

"I won't brother."

"Make sure you finish that novel. I want to see it on the best sellers list." (I also want to see her death in the news paper.)

"For sure, keep your head up."

CHAPTER TEN
"Driving south on I-95"

Savannah and the kids arrived in Maryland around six o'clock Saturday morning. Marcus's parents were up cooking breakfast with the anticipation of their arrival. The kids were going to stay with them for two weeks. Then alternate with her parents for two weeks. Then back to Marcus's parents and so on, for the summer. Savannah was so grateful to have in-laws and parents that didn't mind spending so much time with their grand kids. After breakfast, she kissed and hugged her boys and said her good-byes, before leaving for her parent's house in White Plains. Her dad was gone on a business trip, and wouldn't be back until the following week. So she took her mom to get a manicure and pedicure, before taking her to lunch. After lunch, they did some needed clothes shopping. Once back at her parent's house she laid down for a couple of hours to get some rest before her journey back to North Carolina. Her plan was to leave around eleven-thirty or twelve, that night. She preferred to do the six-hour drive at night, especially in the summer months when it was cooler and less traffic on the roads.

*****

Driving south on I-95 toward North Carolina, she thought about what Andrew had told her, about Ricky's friend Peewee. She looked at her cell phone and remembered she had it turned off all day; she turned it on to check to see if anyone had called. There were three messages, one from her cousin Lushanna and two from her best friends; Desha and Tynesha also known as the A-Team. Even though Savannah name doesn't end with 'A', it sound like it did, so she fell into that group.

Savannah

They acquired the nick name while serving a tour of duty in Iraq. Every time the fella's saw them coming back after two days from being in the field, they would say, "Get out the way, A-Team is coming through."

The "A" team consisted of Savannah's cousin Lushanna Brown. Desha Thompson from the nation's capital, she is a brown skinned beauty about five-five, who wears her hair in a style, like Nia Long; that seems never to be out of place. She has those child bearing hips and a booty that drives the fella's crazy, every time she put on a pair of jeans or form fitting dress. Desha is finishing up her degree at Georgetown. She established three high end hair salons in partnership with her good friend. Thus far, her clients have been actress, senator's wives and a couple of congresswoman to name a few. She also has written a book about true friendship, which made the New York Times best sellers list. She definitely has the Midas touch.

Tynesha is from Brownsville, Brooklyn; by way of Nassau Bahamas. She's also five-five, the slimmest of the bunch, but shapely. She would be a shoe-in winner for America's Top Model, if they weren't looking for skin and bones. This sexy woman has the looks of a goddess, a walk that commands attention, and the commercial ability it takes to be on the hottest magazines in the country. She had graduated from the Fashion Institute of Technology in Manhattan about a year ago. This lady has major skills in the acting and designing department. She had a small role in the HBO movie 'Life Support, with Queen Latifah." When she was in the service, she made four recruiting posters and two commercials for the Air Force. She's also a co-owner of a couple of talent agencies, one in New York, and one in California.

The "A" team, were known for being the sexiest woman with hard core combat experience. Savannah love them because, not only do their chemistry's mix, but they are there for one another at any given moment. When Savannah was laid up in the hospital, they took time off from their busy schedules and family life taking turns staying with her, until the day she was released.

Savannah was so happy they left messages saying they're coming to North Carolina next month to spend time with her while the kids were gone for the summer. That was news that made her day.

Not only were these women beautiful, intelligent and successful, they can be lethal if backed into a corner. By the grace of God they all were stationed at Tallil Air Base, just outside Nasiriyah, Iraq, about a hundred and ninety miles south of Baghdad. They were always able to stay close to each other. Even though Tynesha was doing commercials for the Air Force, they were assigned to an Information Operations Squadron. The four of them were chosen because of their backgrounds and training to go on certain missions. These were not assignments that you would see on any training films, or hear about on World News Tonight, only a select few and the four of them along with the ground commander of Special Forces were assigned to these kinds of units. They were careful not to send them out more than two days at a time, because of the intensity and time allotted to complete the mission. Some of their missions included killing people up close and personal, with their bare hands. They were highly trained assassins. The ladies had enough of the killing business, so when their enlistment was up, they decided to depart the service with honorable discharges. Savannah prayed she didn't have to ever go in that bag of talent again, but she had no choice when her husband was murdered.

Savannah was very excited to see her girls again and so desperately needed them for support and to bring some stability back in her life. They've been through a lot and they are the only ones who would truly understand her actions, without judging her. She knew one thing for sure; they were going to be mad as hell with her, because she didn't call them to assist her. The only one that knew anything in the group was her cousin Shanna. She didn't want her cousin deeply involved, due to fear of another family member getting killed. To look at her friends, you would never think they were action junkies, but they lived for the moment. Savannah thought, if she take them out to have a good time, their first night in North Carolina, they wouldn't be so hard on her.

CHAPTER ELEVEN
"Chi-B took the microphone"

It was early August, when the ladies arrived. Savannah filled them in on what she did in the name of vengeance. They were upset with her, like she thought they would be, because she didn't call them to assist her. Savannah explained to them it was personal and she had to do it alone. She also promised them that if anything else was to jump-off, she would inform them and ask for their assistance. That night Savannah took them to a club, downtown were her friends Chi-B and Masta G were performing. They were in town on a stateside tour from Japan. They called Savannah, when they got in town and left her some VIP tickets. The ladies were seated at a table right up front. Seeing Chi-B and Masta-G perform again was so fulfilling, it been six years since she saw them last. Chi-B took the microphone and in a soft yet eloquent Japanese accent, said. "I would like to thank you all for coming out and showing us some U.S. love. This next single is off our album 'Taxi 2009' called "Satisfaction Guaranteed" I would like to dedicate this song to my girl, Savannah and her friends. It's been six years since Masta-G and I had seen her." With a smile she pointed at their table. She stood in front of the microphone that was in the stand and began to sing, as Masta-G did his thing, on instrumentals. *"Is it...is it here yet? No I don't see it. Taxi, take me to paradise. Can't you see I'm crying? Taxi, don't get me there too late..."* Savannah and the girls clapped, whistled and threw kisses at her and Masta-G. Then Chi-B broke out rapping in Japanese and the club went wild. Savannah knew they would set it off. Their music is wonderful with a soulful sound.

The atmosphere was wonderful. Savannah was so grateful to be around true friends and family.

Savannah

She and the girls were having a great time and enjoying their surroundings, and guys were sending them drinks trying to get in their Vicky's. If they knew they didn't have a chance with any of the "A" team, they would have saved their dollars. After the show, the girls had a few drinks with Chi-B and Master-G, before saying their good-byes. Chi-B and Masta-G had to catch an early flight to New York for a sold out concert they were performing at Madison Square Garden. They were opening for the Jazz Masters, Keiko Matsui and a host of others. When Savannah and the girls left the club, they were feeling the alcohol, but made it to the house safely and they stayed up two more hours, talking about the night. Seeing her cousin and friends again really made her feel good. She felt truly blessed that they have been in each other's inner circle for so many years and still have so much fun when they got together.

*****

It was seven o'clock in the morning, when Savannah got up and began fixing breakfast. She was going to make a serious spread for her company. The menu consisted of bacon, scrambled eggs, grits, sausage, pancakes, toast, muffins, bagels, assorted fruits, coffee, and orange juice. It's not often she get a chance to do a big breakfast like this, because she doesn't keep much company. The kids don't eat a big breakfast, even though it's the most important meal of the day. Possibly, when they get older they will appreciate mama's breakfast.

It was around seven-thirty, when Desha made her way to the kitchen, wearing nothing but an over sized black tee shirt.

"One of the dead has risen." Savannah spoke out jokingly.

"Good morning, girl." Desha responded as she opened the fridge to retrieve the jar of pink grapefruit juice. "My head is thumpin'." She moaned before sitting down at the kitchen table.

"Shit, you drank enough." Savannah scolded, as she handed Desha a cup and placed the grits on the stove. Holding her forehead with her left hand she responded, "I know, a little too much."

She chuckled while proceeding to pour the juice. A few minutes later, Shanna made her way to the gathering hole and took a seat next to Desha. Shanna reaches for Desha's glass of juice.

"Oh, no you don't!" Desha blurted out, while moving her glass out of reach. Savannah handed her a cup and told her there was plenty of juice and to get her own.

Shanna looked at Desha with puppy dog eyes, before responding. "Where's the love sister?"

"The love is in that sixty-four ounce carton of juice, in front of you." They all started laughing. By this time the food was ready. Savannah placed it on the table. Desha and Shanna retrieved the dishes from the cabinet.

"Good morning everyone." Tynesha, greeted all with a smile. They returned her greetings. They took a hold of each other hands as Savannah blessed the food. They were fixing their plates, when Savannah noticed, how much Tynesha was putting on her plate.

"Tynesha!" Savannah yelled out, and paused for a second. "How come you're the smallest of the bunch, but eat the most? Are you pregnant?"

"No, I'm not pregnant." She replied all nonchalant. "I just have a high metabolism."

"More like a tape worm." Desha interjected. Laughter filled the room.

"Y'all need to shut up and pass me the damn grits." Tynesha smiled.

It was great to see everyone enjoying the food, and laughing as Savannah look around. They talked about everything from American Idol to what was going on in their everyday lives to the latest movies that's out. They hadn't seen each other in over five years, and had a lot of catching up to do. However they stayed in touch by phone and email. As they were finishing up, Shanna said, "Cuz, you put your foot in this breakfast."

Savannah

"You sure did sistah." Tynesha added.

"I second that." Desha cosigned, taking a sip of coffee.

"Well thank you ladies. I'm glad you enjoyed the meal." Savannah replied as she gathered up the dishes. The house phone rang and Shanna picked it up and handed it to Savannah.

"Hello."

"Savannah!" Her mother bellowed sounding as if something was wrong.

"Hay mama, what's going on? Is everything alright?" The girls continued to clean up the kitchen.

"Your father was mugged right in front of the house; a few minutes ago."

"Oh my God, is daddy alright mama?" Everyone's undivided attention was on Savannah, as her mother continued.

"I heard some noise outside the door, so I went to see what the hell was going on and three thugs were on your father. I went to help and one of them pushed me to the ground. Stay down bitch! He yelled at me. I said bitch, while trying to get back on my feet, when one of them threw a piece of paper at me."

"Mama, were you hurt? Are you all right? How about the kids, are they alright?" Savannah was beside herself as she listened to her mother.

"I'm alright baby, and the kids are doing fine. They were crying and upset, but they're calm now."

"What did the note say mama?" Her mother began to talk in a whisper, as if she didn't want someone to hear. "They are looking for you, baby.

"Me! Did you give the note to the deputies?" She was still whispering.

"No, your father wanted to talk to you first." She had reverted back to her normal speaking voice.

"He was hit in the head and may require some stitches. The Sheriff's are here along with EMS, to transport him to the hospital. I'm going to follow them in my car."

"Did you or daddy get a look at who they were?"

"Yeah honey, we both did and gave a description to the deputies. Hold on baby." As Savannah waited for her mother to return, her girls were curious as they stared at her. Within seconds her mother had returned to the phone.

"Honey, one of the deputies just informed me that they caught someone fitting the description I had given them and wanted me to identify them."

"I'm on my way home mama." Before her mother could respond, Savannah hung up the phone. She was pissed, angry and saddened by what had taken place. Her mother and father could have been killed. Savannah relayed the conversation she had with her mother to her girls. They began scrambling for their cell phones making call after call. In between the phone calls, they told Savannah they were coming too. In less than an hour, they were packed and on the road, heading north.

As the ladies were making their way to I-95, Savannah put on her ear piece and called her friend, Valerie Smalls in DC. Valerie and Savannah go back to when they were teenagers living in Detroit. Valerie is one of the sweetest people you could ever meet. She has a lot of connections and doesn't flaunt it. If you didn't know her personally, you would never know how powerful a woman she really is. Savannah had found her number after she did her thing with Ricky; otherwise Valerie could have helped her get the police to do their job.

"Hello Val. This is Savannah."

"Hey Savannah, how are you doing these days?"

"Not too well. Something went down at my parent's house, and I'm on my way to Maryland with some of my friends."

"It's that serious?"

"Yeah, I believe it to be"

"Do you need for me to do anything?"

"I'm not sure Val. I would have to wait until I get there. I hate to ask you for favors and you haven't heard from me in a long time."

"We all get busy baby. I know how it is. Plus you my girl for life, you don't have to worry about needing a favor from me. I got you!"

"I really appreciate that."

"Call me when you get up here, and drive safely."

Savannah

"I will, talk to you later…bye." Savannah tapped her ear piece disconnecting the call. The girls were still on their cells getting everything in order on their end, because of their unexpected trip to Maryland. As they turned onto I-95 heading north, Savannah couldn't help but think that Ricky had something to do with the attack on her parents. Thinking to herself, *I warned that bastard if he ever messed with my people what would happen to him. I guess he don't believe fatback is greasy and fire burn. If he's behind this, I will make sure he understands the meaning of both.* Savannah couldn't contain her thoughts and spoke out loud. "I'm going to destroy that mother fucker." Everyone looked at Savannah, but no one said a word.

CHAPTER TWELVE
"I'm with you until the end"

'You have a collect call from Ricky Fontayne, an inmate at the Colorado State Prison in Florence. If you elect to accept the charges, please press 1 now,' a prerecorded message came across the line. The phone clicked for a few seconds indicating the call was accepted. Knowing the prison administration listened to their conversation, the two used their own code to communicate.

"Hello!"

"Yo, Peewee, what's up?" (Have you located her, yet?)

"Nothing, but the price of gas and taxes." (Not yet, but a message was delivered to her parent's house today.)

"I hear that." (Good job.)

"Yo, I know that shit is hard inside, but if you take one day at a time, and stay positive, you'll be alright." (I expect her presence any day now.)

"All I do is sit in my cell or in the law library and read most of the time." (Do you have someone sitting on the house?)

"Keep reading brother, because it will help pass the time, while keeping you away from the bull shit." (Someone's watching it, as we speak.)

"You're right about that. Alright brother, I'll call from time-to-time. I appreciate you being there." (I'll be checking with you on the progress.)

"Don't worry about it. I'm with you until the end."(Not a problem.)

"I'll check you later."

"Peace."

"Peace."

Savannah

Shortly after Ricky hung up the receiver, the alarm went off, informing the inmates and guards they were going to be put on lock down, and the inmates must leave the day room and go back to their cells. Once back at his six by nine, Ricky's cellmate told him the reason they were getting lock down, was because a "gassing" occurred. Gassing is when an inmate takes urine and feces and put it into a plastic bag and throws it on an unsuspecting guard. Sometimes the act is extended for another inmate.

Survival in this environment is a daily challenge mentally, medically and physically. Your survival depended on you knowing the mix on your own, or somebody showing you the ropes. Either way, you better be a fast learner, if you're going to last more than a week in that type of wilderness. The word mix is another name for prison culture. Prison culture are the do's and don'ts and the who's and who not's, and what guards are bringing the drugs in; and the snitches to stay away from. On any given day, of any given moment at any given hour, your life can come to an end, before you know what happened. Certain inmates know why another inmate is there, before they step on the cell block. The reason being, the guards are friends with certain inmates and they tell them things. The inmates then spread the news, hoping to get that inmate killed or informing the general population, that this is not the man you want to mess with. You also have the snitching inmates that have access to certain location. They hear things and go around the prison as if they are TMZ, hoping to get some favor for passing on information that is not privy to the rest of the inmates.

Since Ricky's short incarceration, he has seen a number of inmates get killed over stupid things. His first day there, an inmate stabbed another because he didn't give him a puff of his cigarette. Another was killed because he spilled some jailhouse alcohol in his cell and the inmates that helped make the mixture didn't get a chance to drink their share. Ricky was caught up in the fracas and almost took another inmate out. He felt he was being disrespected by a loud mouth inmate, as he was having a conversation with several other inmates. Everyone knew about Ricky's pharmaceutical connection on the outside and knew he was the top dog out in the world.

Brooklen Borne

As he was trying to form alliances with the heads of states on the inside along with a few crooked ass guards, the brother felt Ricky was getting all the money when that wasn't the case. In actuality, they were getting paid equally. By splitting things equally it would lessen the chance of a war breaking out over who would control the drug flow in their housing block. Of course there's always the possibility of someone getting greedy or being stupid, and if that's the case they are dealt with accordingly. *What's up with this muthafucka acting like he Farrakhan and shit. Who the fuck this niggah thinks he is?* Ricky said to himself.

Ricky knew he had to do something immediately because his reputation and credibility was on the line. Before the brother could finish his next sentence, Ricky pounced on him with several blows to his head and throat. The other inmates sat at the table as if nothing had occurred. Within minutes it was over. The guards never saw the commotion on camera, all they saw was an inmate on the ground bleeding. The beaten inmate was taken to the prison infirmary for his injuries. Without any pressure from the prison officials he snitched on Ricky, who was promptly sent to the hole for two weeks. Ricky didn't mind at all. Because his prison status raised a few more points among the inmates. Moreover, not only did it seal his reputation as a bad ass that was fair in business dealings and will hurt you if you crossed him, it boosted his ego. After Ricky's two weeks in the hole, he came looking for the snitch, only to find out that he was in the morgue with a toe tag. The beaten inmate opened his mouth one too many times and paid the ultimate price.

CHAPTER THIRTEEN
"What's going on?"

It was early in the morning when Savannah and her friends arrived in Maryland. The sun hadn't fully risen and they were about a block away from her parent's house, when an uncomfortable feeling came over her; that something just wasn't right.

"Pull over!" she shouted, sitting up in the seat.

"What?"

"Pull over!" Savannah repeated looking at Shanna. Shanna pulled to the right and brought the car to a stop.

"What's wrong? What's up? What's going on?" everyone in the car began asking. Savannah explained to them that she had a gut feeling this was a set up.

"A set up! Shit! By who?" Tynesha asked, with a confused look on her face.

"I'm not sure!" Savannah responded. "It's hard to explain, but the feeling is too strong." Desha suggested that her and Shanna should get out and walk down the block, while Tynesha and Savannah enter the block from the opposite direction. With the women entering the block from opposite directions, Desha and Shanna would be able to get a jump on anyone, who was lying in wait for them.

"What if they have guns and shit, then what? Because we don't have any fire power to even out the situation; if a shootout occurs." Shanna blurted as if to say, come up with another plan. Applying a fresh coat of lip-gloss, Savannah told everyone to relax, as she thought of a plan.

"Don't think too long, because I'm ready to put my foot in someone's ass," Desha said impatiently.

"If these people are bent on hurting your family in the worst way, then we are going to need more than our fist," Tynesha added.

Savannah

"Tee's right." Savannah uttered as she began to dial Valerie's number.

"Are you in town yet?" Valerie answered the call, without a hello.

"Yeah, we just got here. We're parked around the corner from the house; but I have a strong feeling that something isn't right. I'm really worried."

"Where's your location?"

"We are parked at the corner of Fern and Foster, in the Kings View Sub Division."

"What are you driving?"

"I'm in an Ocean Mist Blue BMW 745, with personalized NC tags; that read MIN8IVE."

"Hang tight. I'll have someone there in thirty minutes. Whatever you do, don't you or your friends go down that block. You hear me!"

"I hear you,"

After hanging up, Shanna looked at Savannah and asked "What's up?"

"We wait," she replied, putting her head back against the headrest and closing her eyes. Thirty minutes later a Black Navigator with tinted windows pulled alongside the ladies vehicle. The passenger window slowly rolled down, revealing two handsome African American men. As if on cue, the back passenger window followed suit, exposing two handsome Latino men. The ladies immediately got a sugar rush. The four men were dressed in the latest street wear, and wearing Oakley sunglasses.

"Which one of you is Savannah?" The driver asked.

"I am," Savannah answered with a blank expression.

"Valerie sent us. She filled us in on your possible situation; that you may have some unwanted company."

"Yeah, that's right." One of the men reached out the window and handed Shanna, a small flat screen devise and told Savannah to plug it into the car power outlet. She did as instructed. He then told her to press the middle button and then type in the numbers 745, the model of her car. An image appeared on the screen, showing their exact location. Desha and Tynesha leaned over the seats to get a view of the screen.

"We're going to cruise up the block and you'll see everything that we see. If someone is carrying a weapon, the screen will automatically go into a thermo image and identify what is being carried and where it's located on the person or in the vehicle. You will also be able to hear what we are saying," the driver informed.

The SUV pulled off, and the women immediately turned their attention to the screen. About midway up the block on the right hand side was a Burgundy Escalade, with three people inside. The screen changed like he said it would. The three occupants in the Escalade were carrying AK-47's and the AK's were located in the rear section of the vehicle. A few seconds later, the screen went black.

"I could use one of these in my ride," Desha said, as they all shook their heads in agreement.

The four men circled the block and pulled back alongside Savannah's car. The driver exited the SUV and positioned himself between the two vehicles. He had to be about six-four, with a muscular physique. He was built like a Greek God. Matter of fact all the men were built like Greek God's.

"Ladies as you saw on the monitor, Savannah's gut feeling was right. This is what we are going to do. You will stay in your car until we eliminate the threat. Once we pull away, it will be safe for you to go to your parents' home. Expect a call from Ms. Smalls, with some vital information, understood!" Savannah shook her head, indicating she did. He then asked Shanna would she be so kind to retrieve the monitor. Shanna, placed the device into his hand and not wanting to let go, slightly pulling his hand towards her bosom, but not quite touching them; before letting his hand go. He paused for a second and smiled at her, before returning to his vehicle. The girls all thought Shanna was going to have an orgasm right there on the spot.

Once the women were out of the drivers hearing range, Tynesha asked, "Do you have any dignity, with your fast ass self?" Before Shanna could respond, Desha added. "Oh shut up girl, if you

Savannah

had the chance, your hot ass probably would have done the same thing." They all began to laugh.

Savannah still chuckling said. "It's getting hot in here." The four Greek Gods as the ladies referred to them, pulled up next to the Escalade, and tossed something inside. The Escalade lit up as if a flash bang had been thrown inside. The Greek Gods pulled away and another black van pulled next to the Escalade and two white guys jumped out and removed the occupants, and placed them into the van. No sooner than the van sped off, a dark skinned brother that was walking down the block jumped into the Escalade and pulled away.

"Oh shit! Did you see that?" Shanna said aloud with excitement.

"I sure did." Savannah replied feeling relieved, the threat was no longer there.

"Those guys rolled like they were from that T.V. series The Unit." Tynesha added. Shanna started the car, and drove toward the house. Once inside, Savannah checked to see if her mom and dad were there. There was a note from her mom on the sofa table. She opened it and the note read, they were at the hospital and that her dad wasn't feeling so well. The ladies quickly freshened up, before leaving for the hospital.

As they were walking out the house, Savannah's cell phone rang. It was Valerie. Savannah closed and locked the front door, while the rest of the girls looked on.

"The people that were sitting on your parent's home work for a guy name, Peewee. Does that name sound familiar to you?"

"No!"

"Well, Peewee is doing a favor for a guy named Ricky Fontayne, who is in federal lock up."

"Ricky, I was afraid of that," she responded pissed off, knowing Ricky's ass was going to be hers.

"So what are the likes of those characters doing outside your parent's house?" Savannah went on to tell her the whole story about what happened to her and Marcus, and how she retaliated against them.

"Oh, my Lord, Savannah, I remember seeing it all over the news. I didn't pay much attention, because the media like to hype things up for ratings."

"Yeah, I went for revenge until I got a hold of Ricky. I'm the one that sent his punk ass up the river."

"Why are you telling me this now? I could have helped you ma. The only thing that changed about me is my life status Savannah. I had your back when we were kids and I have your back now." Valerie relayed her thoughts like a caring older sister. "You're my girl and I don't know what I would do if anything would happen to you or the kids."

"I knew I could handle it. So I did something about it."

"I understand honey. But don't you hesitate if you need back up of any kind." There was silence. "YOU HEAR ME!" Valerie said, raising her voice as she ended the conversation.

"I hear you, Val." Savannah responded like a little girl. When she got off the phone Desha looked at her and asked,

"Who were those guys?"

Before Savannah could respond, Tynesha cut her off and asked, "Who is Valerie?" Shanna looked unconcerned. The ladies weren't known to keep secrets from each other, and mindful of this, Savannah told them.

"Valerie is my girl from the Detroit days. She works for the C.I.A now. I guess those guys work for her." Smiling, the girls gave Savannah a hug as she was about to open the door to the car. Shanna then looked at the girls and said, "Valerie's no joke, huh?"

"No, she's the real deal," Savannah responded, taking the keys from Shanna and told her that she would drive.

"Savannah!" Desha spoke in a firm voice.

"Yeah, what's up?"

"You know Rickey, Peewee and whoever else that are mixed up in this mess are going to have to leave this world, as we know it. You know where I'm coming from?

"With a body count as long as yours, I know where you coming from. I was just praying that I didn't have to go back there ladies. It's a dark place, a very dark place." No one said another word. They drove in silence, each with their own thoughts.

CHAPTER FOURTEEN
"Her hair was cut in a Bob style"

Savannah was speeding down Branch Avenue as if it was her own private road; heading towards Southern Maryland Hospital Center. Once she arrived, she jumped out and rushed through the emergency entrance; while the other's waited in the car. *I can't stand hospitals,* she thought as she entered the building. She stopped at the information desk and asked the white lady who wore too much make up and a hair do from the fifties, sitting behind the desk; on the phone. Out of respect, Savannah waited a few minutes until the lady finished her conversation. Listening attentively to the woman on the phone, Savannah could hear it was a personal call of non important.

"Excuse me. My father, Mr. Irving Carrington was brought in earlier today by ambulance; what room can I find him in?" The expression the woman gave Savannah, was one of, how dare you interrupt my conversation; are you crazy? The woman kept staring at Savannah, as if she was beneath her; as she continued her conversation. Savannah gave her a look that could have killed half the staff in the hospital. She then commenced to jumping in the woman's butt with both feet. When she finished with that woman, the lady got the message that Savannah was not the one, she can practice her higher than mighty attitude and tough look on. Savannah finished by saying, "All I want to know is what room my fathers' located at. Why must I have to go through this nonsense, because you want to shoot the shit on the phone?" The woman's attitude changed, and she eagerly directed Savannah to the location of her father.

Devin and Chance, were sitting quietly on some chairs, which was located just outside the room. When they saw their mother, they leaped from their resting spot and came running to give their mommy a big hug. Savannah smile and gave multiple kisses all over their faces. "I just love my little men." She boasted still kissing and hugging them.

Savannah

After supplying them both with some motherly love, she told them to sit back down while she goes see grandpa. Her well mannered boys did what they were told and they sat down without incident. When she entered the room, her mother was helping her father put on his shirt. She looked up and saw Savannah and a big smile appeared on her face. Savannah walked up to her and gave her a big hug. "Hey baby girl." Her father said, excited. She then turned her attention toward him and gave her dad a hug, before asking him was he alright? And how many stitches did he have to get, to close the wound on the side of his head?

"It took thirteen, but I'm alright. After coming back home, I got dizzy and your mother insisted we go back; to see why I was feeling so dizzy. The doctors took x-rays and did test on me and told your mother and me, that everything was alright. The doctor said I raised my head up too fast, causing the dizziness. It's common after getting stitches where I got them. But everything is good now, and I'm cleared to go home." Her mother came over and placed her arm around Savannah shoulder's and asked.

"Have you seen the boys?"

"Yes, I did mom. I saw my two handsome men." She answered as she helped her father off the bed. A nurse's aide came in with a wheel chair. She was a brown skinned sister around eighteen years old. Her hair was cut in a bob style and she wore very little make up. Savannah liked her professional but sassy look.

"I don't need a wheel chair darling. I've been here all morning and I'm ready to walk out this place."

"I know Mr. Carrington, but its procedure." The young lady responded with a smile, as she helped Mr. Carrington into the wheel chair. She rolled him out the room, while Savannah collected her sons as they all headed towards the elevator. Once in the lobby, Savannah told Devin and Chance to ride back with their cousin Shanna, while she rode back with grandma and grandpa. After she got her parents' settled in the car she informed them on who was behind the attack; but didn't tell them her plans to retaliate. Her parent's took the news in stride when her father said. "Let's stop and get something to eat." Savannah and her mother started laughing. "Nothing is going to stop your father from getting something to eat baby." Mrs. Carrington could hardly get the words out, because she was laughing so hard. *It's so good to hear my mother laugh.* Savannah thought, as she continued to laugh as well.

"Mom, what happened to the guy, they brought you around to identify?"

"It was the wrong man."

"That's typical." Savannah mumbled as she leaned back in the seat. Savannah couldn't believe what was inside her head. She would not imagine in a million years, the thoughts she was having. She knew if her husband was still alive, her mind wouldn't be so dark. Now that he's gone, she's thinking like an Angela Jolie in one of action movies. She and her girls, have an unofficial license to kill, with extreme prejudice; by any means necessary.

CHAPTER FIFTEEN
"Savannah, what's the game plan?"

    After getting some fish and shrimp from Trips Seafood on Crain Highway, they headed home. Savannah and the girls stayed the night at her parent's house since her parent's had the room for them. Besides, her parent's loved the company. Not wanting any fish or shrimp, Desha ordered some Chinese food for those that didn't want to eat seafood. Savannah played Wii bowling with her boys until the food arrived; then they went down stairs, to the finished basement. It had a full size bar, professional pool table, 60 inch plasma theater system, full bathroom, bed room, pull out couch, refrigerator, kitchen table and enough room so that nothing was cluttered. Her parents' basement is bigger than most people apartments. After the food arrived, Savannah fixed the kids their plates and walked them upstairs to sit at the kitchen table. When she came back down stairs, Shanna asked her, what the game plan was.

    "Well the first thing I'm going to do is make contact with Karyn, and see if she will help in squashing this mess."

    "Who's Karyn?" Tynesha inquired while taking a cap off a bottle of Corona.

    "She is Ricky's ex-wife." Savannah replied getting a couple of beer glasses out the cabinet.

    "Do you really think she's going to help?" Desha asked while getting plates for everyone.

    "I don't know, but I'm going to give it a shot."

    "Well she did stay clear of everything that was going down." Shanna added.

    "If we can end this situation before it gets out of hand, so be it." Tynesha said coming out the bathroom from washing her hands.

    "My trust level outside this circle is very thin, so it's best to have a backup plan just in case somebody doesn't want to use common sense." Desha said as she took a seat at the table.

Savannah

Knowing the people they may be dealing with, they couldn't be walking around blind. While they ate, Savannah devised a plan along with eight rules, they all were familiar with.

Rule One: Use only the time needed to eliminate the threat, because every second will count.
Rule Two: Avoid hurting innocent people, at all cost.
Rule Three: Have more than one escape route.
Rule Four: Communicate with one another throughout the mission.
Rule Five: Stick strictly to the plan, unless you have no choice to divert.
Rule Six: Do everything possible, to ensure we don't have any fatalities.
Rule Seven: If we do have a fatality, no one gets left behind. No matter what!
Rule Eight: In case something goes wrong, implement plan B without any thought or hesitation.

"First, I would try to talk to Karyn, to see if she would assist us in ending this potentially explosive situation peacefully. Second, if she's not willing to help, be prepared to go after Peewee with everything we can muster up. Third, protect my family at all cost while this mission is active. Fourth, keep my sons from knowing what's going on. They don't need to be worrying about me. Losing their father took a big enough toll on them already. Fifth, stay two steps ahead of the police; not revealing our identity or leaving any evidence, leading back to us. And last but not lease, May Jesus cover us in his blood." They all bowed their heads after Savannah's speech and said "Amen."

CHAPTER SIXTEEN
"I know your story"

     Savannah contacted Karyn the next day and explained to her briefly, what had happened to caused the ugly situation between her and Ricky. Karyn could hear Savannah's pain and invited her to her home for a sit down. An hour later, Savannah was standing at her door step. Just before ringing the door bell, she adjusted her automatic in her waist band; in case something jumped off. She placed a piece of double mint gum in her mouth, and rang the bell. Karyn opened the door, wearing a lovely print sundress and a pair of Jack Rogers sandals.
     "You must be Savannah?"
     "Yes, I am."
     "Please, come inside. Can I get you anything to drink?"
     "No, thank you." Savannah didn't want to take any chances of her drink being spiked. Both ladies proceed to the living room and made themselves comfortable on the couch. Karyn lived in a five bedroom, four and a half bath, and colonial style brick home in the affluent section of Charles County, in southern Maryland.
     "Karyn, I want to thank you for having a sit down with me." Savannah said, getting comfortable on the couch.
     "I heard a little bit of your story, and I don't know if I could have held up as well and as long as you did. When I found out what Ricky had done to you, I moved out. I'm not going to lie, I still love him and I miss him; but I wasn't living in his crazy world any longer.
     "How did you hear about my story?" Savannah asked with a curious expression.
     "The streets talk, if you listen carefully. But you already know that." Karyn responded taking a sip of coffee.
     "Is it safe to say, you still keep in contact with Ricky?"

Savannah

"I do." Karyn responded, without any hesitation.

"My understanding is that Ricky wants Peewee to do him a favor and that favor is to get me back for sending him to prison. Peewee sent some people over to my parent's house and smacked my mother and father around. Needless to say, the men he sent will not breathe the air of life again."

"Peewee never mentioned anything like that to me and I saw him the other day at the mall." Not revealing she saw him at the prison, when she visited Ricky.

"Karyn, could you please try to convince Peewee this is not his fight. As a matter of fact, a fight does not exist. He did what he did to me first and I retaliated. I didn't ask him to send hit men to my home and kill my husband and by the grace of God my life was spared, and I was shot seven times. All I want is to raise my children in a peaceful environment, and for my parent's to grow old; loving and spending time with their grandchildren. My parents don't need to be getting knocked around for him trying to get back at me; for something that suppose to be squashed. Enough bloodshed has been spilled"

"I feel where you're coming from. Even though Ricky and I didn't produce any children, during our union; he has a daughter that I am close with; so I do understand. I'll give Peewee a call, then I'm out the picture. I'm going to cut Ricky and Peewee out of my world. Just like you did, and move on with my life."

"Thank you Karyn." Savannah expressed her appreciation as they both stood up and gave one another a hug. Then Savannah departed. After closing the front door, Karyn walked toward the kitchen, just as she placed her empty glass in the sink, the phone rang.

"Hello."
"Hey lady!"
"Who's this?"
"It's Peewee."
"You're going to live a long time. Guess who left my house and wanted me to contact you?"
"I don't have a clue. Tell me!"
"Savannah!"

"Get the fuck outta here."

"I'm serious."

"I've been trying to catch up with that lovely lady, for awhile now. Do you have a number, that I can contact her?"

"Yeah, but I'm not going to give it to you."

"Why not?"

"She wants me to inform you, that she doesn't have a beef with you. She just wants to be left alone to raise her children in peace. She said the conflict she had was between her and Ricky. He killed her husband for no reason, so she sent him to prison for it."

"It's more to the story, than just what she told you."

"Okay, I'll give you her number and you two hash it out. But I'm telling you Peewee; don't keep me in the middle of this bull shit. You hear me!"

"I wouldn't do that to you Karyn."

"I'm serious Peewee. You sent your boys after her mother and father to get back at her. You know you're going about this in the wrong way. I feel where she is coming from."

"Savannah sent your man away for a long time."

"My man killed her husband for no reason. She didn't start this shit, but she's capable of finishing it though."

"I bet she didn't tell you everything."

"Like what Peewee?"

"Did you know she was screwing Ricky, when he was with you? She wanted him to leave you and he wouldn't, so she cut off his shit?" A silence came over the phone.

"She was fuckin' him when we were together?"

" The reason Ricky went after them, was because she owed him some money. After the shooting, Savannah promised to pay him in full when she healed. Instead of paying him, she went over to his house to set him up and killed Bruce in the process." Peewee was lying through his teeth. He would say anything to keep Karyn on his side; especially since he's been trying to get in between her legs. Karyn became furious. It was a total silence.

"Karyn are you still there?"

"Yeah, I'm still here. No I didn't know that she was fuckin' him on the regular. She didn't say anything about that."

Savannah

"Do you really think she's going to say something about that to you? Be careful of that Bitch Karyn."

"Peewee why now? Why would you tell me some shit like this?"

"I just thought you should know who you are dealing with."

"He's guilty as much as she is." Karyn replied, even though she was upset.

"That bitch also said she would put your ass to sleep, to get back at Ricky; if need be." Peewee lied some more, knowing he had to say something to push her over the top. He could read Karyn like a book and manipulate her anyway he wanted.

"If what you say is true, why she didn't try to take me out, when she had the chance?"

"Yo, you think she's stupid? She probably was getting a feel for you, to see if you would be an easy target or not."

"Well, that not going to happen and I'll be ready, if she decide to get stupid. Alright Peewee thanks; I'll talk to you later."

"Peace baby girl." Karyn hangs up the phone and leaned back and muttered. Savannah has another problem to worry about now…me!"

CHAPTER SEVENTEEN
"We arrived at five guys..."

      Savannah and Desha were on their way to her parents' house to check on her father, when her cell began to vibrate. Savannah looked to see who was calling her. The cell read no data, so she let it go into voice mail. A few minutes later she checked the voice mail to listen to the message. It was messages from some guy, saying meet him at seven-thirty tonight at Five Guys. This particular Five Guys he wanted to meet her at is located in Waldorf, off Crain Highway; in Saint Charles Plaza. It's a fast food place, which serves hamburgers, hot dogs and fries. The message ended with "It's in reference to Ricky." Savannah immediately passed the information to Desha. Desha pulled out her cell and called Shanna and Tynesha, to inform them of the message.

*****

      Savannah spent most of the day playing with her sons and talking to her father while Desha chilled with Savannah's mom. Her mother had prepared a lovely dinner and ate as a family before they left. Her mother sent two plates back with them for Shanna and Tynesha. They left Savannah parents' place around four o'clock, heading back to Shanna's to get ready for the meeting, with the mysterious voice.
      They arrived at Five Guys around seven twenty-five and sat at a table away from the door and window; just in case they had to make a hasty exit, through the back door. Two guys dressed in the latest street gear, which looked to be about thirty, walked in and sat at the table next to them.
"Which one of you is Savannah?" asked the taller one.

Savannah

Savannah responded, "Why was this meeting set?" Desha added "Because we don't have all night." The way Desha and Savannah answered back, kept the two guys confused on which one of the two ladies was Savannah. It's a technique they used all the time, back in the day.

"Karyn sent us."

"Why didn't she call and meet us?" Desha asked suspiciously.

"She didn't want any more calls on her phone bill that could tie her to Savannah. That's like a safe guard in case the police want to snoop around. Karyn wanted us to let Savannah know, she has information in regards to Peewee putting a hit on her." Savannah looked over at Desha feeling a little uneasy, but decided to play this little game out; to see where it was going to lead them. One of the guys continued to say, while his partner just stared at Desha. "We are going to escort both of you to her, for security reasons; since we don't know which one of you is Savannah. I'll ride with you and you will ride with my boy." He instructed with cold eyes, as he pointed his finger at Desha.

"If you or your boy tries to pull any shit, I'm telling you now it will be your last." Desha said as she leaned toward the guy that was doing all the talking. His boy chuckle at what Desha had just said. Not being phase by what was just told to him, he replied. "Let's go!" and turned to walk out the door. When the four of them stepped out of the establishment, Savannah paused, stopping everyone in their tracks. She signaled Shanna and Tynesha, by running her fingers through her hair, and placing a peppermint in her mouth. The two were in another car for back-up and saw when the men pulled up. Shanna and Tynesha exited the vehicle walked past Savannah's car; while Tynesha walked past the car the two men came in and placed tracking devices in the wheel well. Savannah still had that feeling this was a set up. Savannah kept thinking to herself. If this is for security reasons, she could have came and met us some where more secluded or public.

The house they arrived at wasn't the same one she met with Karyn earlier. Savannah asked the guy. "Is this where Karyn live?"

Being that she already knew the answer. "No this is one of our safe houses." When they entered the house, all hell broke loose. The guy Desha rode with, turned around and sucker punched her in the jaw, knocking her to the floor. When she hit the floor, her eyes were closed and her body was limp, she seemed to be knocked out. Savannah advanced toward the guy that hit Desha, when the guy she walked in with, pointed a pistol at her head and told her, "Go ahead bitch! Go ahead!" Savannah stopped in her tracks and didn't say a word. She just stared him in his eyes. "Well bitch, don't just stare at me do something. So I can blow your fuckin' face off." The intense moment was broken buy another voice in the room.

"I finally get a chance to meet Shauntay Justice. I apologize; your correct name is Savannah Carrington." Savannah looked to her left. It was Peewee. He was wearing a white shirt, blue slacks, blue socks and no shoes. He slowly strolled down the stairs and signaled to one of his boys and said "Pick that bitch up off the floor and place her on the couch. Ms Carrington, you can have a seat next to her." Savannah did as she was told. She sat next to Desha and took a hold of her hand. Unnoticeably to the others, Desha squeezed her hand three times, letting her know that she wasn't knocked out. Savannah felt relieved. Peewee continued, while his associate kept his gun aimed at Savannah's head. "Did you really think it would be so easy to get next to me? I guess you wanted to cut my shit off too." He said as he walked closer to Savannah.

"Look! I want this shit to end. I wasn't coming after you. I wanted peace between us. Enough craziness has gone down already." Savannah responded.

"If you want peace, then I want something from you." He then unzipped his pants and pulled out his penis. Savannah looked at him like he had lost his damn mind, as she leaned away from him. He smiled at her and grabbed the back of head, with a fist full of her hair and slapped her in the face with his dick. Savannah jumped up and caught him in the jaw with a right cross, before his associate pistol slapped her in the mouth. Savannah fell back onto the couch, bleeding from the lip.

"Fuck!" She yelled out, as pain overwhelmed her head.

Savannah

"You're pretty quick Savannah." He admired, while rubbing the side of his face.

"Let's go one on one and I'll show you how quick I am." Savannah replied while blood oozed from the gash on her lip.

"You're a feisty one. I like your kind."

"Yeah, your punk ass boy Ricky liked me too."

"For a favor to Ricky, this is what's going to happen. Me and the fellas, (pointing to the other associates in the room.) are going to fuck the shit out of you and your unconscious pussy partner. Then after a couple of days of dickin' you two down, I'm going to cut both your arms off, followed by your legs."

"So you need your boys." Savannah said, as she sat up. "You can't do it your fuckin' self?" One of the associates grabbed Savannah around the neck and was choking her. She began to ease her left hand to lower back, for her piece that was in her waist band.

"Bitch I'll take the pussy now." Peewee hollered as he started to walk toward her; when all of a sudden Desha jumped up, pulling a .38 snub nose from her boot and began shooting, taking out the guy closest to Peewee. Savannah couldn't believe the dumb asses, didn't check them for weapons. Shanna and Tynesha were observing the scene through a window, all along. They shot through the opened window taking out the rest of Peewee's crew; those boys didn't know what had hit them; because Shanna and Tynesha used silencers with laser aiming modules. Savannah had her automatic aimed at Peewee's head. Desha opened the front door to let Tynesha and Shanna in. Savannah instructed them to go check out the rest of the house; while Desha and her dealt with Peewee. Tynesha went to the basement and Shanna went up stairs. The surprised look on Peewee's face, with his hands in the air said it all…it was priceless. The sight of him almost made Savannah laugh.

Desha took Savannah's face in her hand to get a closer look at her busted lip, before walking over to a nearby mirror, to take a look at her jaw. She had a serious bruise forming. She put her gun away and walked over to Peewee and kicked him in the groan. He dropped to his knees holding his private area, she then pistol slapped him a couple of times; before saying "Who's the pussy partner now bitch?"

"Basements' clear." Tynesha said as she stood by Savannah. Shanna was coming down the stairs with company.

"Who's that?" Savannah asked, while Desha used police plastic flex cuffs to bound Peewee feet and hands behind his back.

"I found her hiding in the closet in one of the rooms." Shanna informed all, as she tossed the woman to the floor. The woman was about five-two, a hundred and fifteen pounds, dark in complexion and her skin was flawless. She wasn't a pretty lady, but did have some beauty about her. She was wearing some lovely tan slacks, a beautiful brown blouse and sandals. Tapping the woman on the head, with the barrel of the glock, Shanna asked her why she was hiding in the closet.

"I'm his sister." The woman responded, looking over at Peewee. Continuing she added. "I don't approve of his life style and have been trying to get him to do right." Then she began to cry.

"I can imagine having to deal with a stupid ass brother like him on a daily bases." Savannah said, almost sympathizing with her. Thump! Savannah conversation was cut short; Tynesha had shot the woman in the neck. Savannah looked at Tynesha for some kind of answer on why she had shot the woman.

"She was reaching for a gun." Tynesha said, pointing at the woman. Savannah looked back at the woman holding her neck, as blood gushed from the hole with every beat of her heart and with the other hand, on her ankle revealing a derringer.

"I'm going to get you bitch's, if that's the last thing I do!" Peewee screamed out. "You ain't getting shit. Shut up!" Shanna replied as she slapped Peewee upside the head with her gun, knocking him out.

"Look-a here, look-a here!" Desha said as she pulled a duffle bag full of money, from the closet in the foyer. Savannah commanded Shanna and Tynesha to pick Peewee up off the floor, so they can leave before someone else show up.

"What about her?" Tynesha asked.

"Fuck her, let her bleed out." Savannah replied, as they closed the front door behind them.

Savannah

Shanna and Tynesha had put Peewee in the trunk, placing a strip of tape across his mouth, before shutting the trunk.

As they drove away from the house, Savannah noticed a car pulling out behind them. Savannah turned left driving north on Bensville Road. The car behind them did the same. She slowed down, they slowed down. She sped up, they sped up.
"Do you think they are some of Peewee's people?" Desha asked.

"I don't know, but we are going to find out in a few minutes." Savannah responded as she divided her attention on the road in front of them and the suspicious vehicle tailing behind. Desha removed her gun from her waist band and placed it on her lap. Savannah pulled out her cell and called Tynesha, and Shanna to inform them what was going on. They were driving ahead of them.

"Hold on, we'll swing around and come up behind them."
"No, we'll handle this. We don't want to get caught up in the crossfire." Savannah, shouted back. "Just keep going and well meet up at the spot. Make sure no one see you bringing Peewee inside."

"Alright, catch up with you in a few. You two be safe." Shanna said before, speeding away, creating distance.
Desha had loaded the two glocks that was underneath the seat, then tapped Savannah on the shoulder.

"Stop the car, I will jump out and see what their problem is."

"Desha, if I stopped the car and you jump out, there will be no cover between you and them. They will be able to pick you off like fish in a barrel. Besides, we don't know if they are friend or foe. I should be able to lose them between here and B-more, so buckle up." Savannah turned onto route 228, heading towards 210/Indianhead Highway. The car behind them did the same; now they are tailing a little closer. A quarter mile up, Savannah veered right onto 210 and picked up speed; the car behind them, mirrored their every move.

"I believe they are following us to see where we are going." Desha said as she looked back.

"I don't think so, because they wouldn't be following us this close. If they wanted to see where we were going, that would back off and not make themselves so obvious." Savannah replied as she looked in the rear view mirror. One slight advantage Savannah had, her windows were limousine tinted and they couldn't see in her car. Both cars were moving at a pretty high rate of speed, luckily the green lights were in her favor.

"At least they aren't shooting at us." Desha said nonchalantly. No sooner than she got the words out her mouth, they began shooting. Savannah couldn't believe they were shooting at them. Savannah stepped on the gas trying to get some distance between them, as they exceeded speeds over a hundred miles per hour. Bobbing and weaving, zigging and zagging, she just knew they were going to get the police attention or at the least someone calling in their erratic driving. On any given day there is an abundance of P.G. County and State troopers or any other law enforcement agencies on this stretch of road. Savannah knew she had to shake this car. A bullet whizzed through the rear window shattering it, and exiting out the front. Another bullet took out the passenger side view mirror.

"Come on Savannah, shake these mutha fucker's." Desha hollered, as she lowered herself in the seat. They were quickly approaching the 95/495/Indian Head divide, Savannah knew she had to do something fast. She lowered the windows and opened the moon roof.

"You know what I'm getting ready to do, so I advise you to brace yourself." As they passed the last light before the divide, Savannah slammed on the brakes, turned the wheel and spun the car around; a hundred and eighty degrees.
Now facing the pursuing car, but now driving backward. They unbuckled and Savannah leaned out the window, and Desha stood up through the moon roof; and they began firing at the car. The pursuing car windshield was hit several times. The car swerved to the right then to the left; hitting the Jersey wall. The car went into a tumble, sending debris everywhere, before coming to a rest on its roof. Savannah spun the car back around just in time to exit off; onto 95/495 North.

"That's what I'm talking about. You can drive your ass off when you want too." Desha yelled excitedly damn near jumping into Savannah lap to give her a kiss on the cheek.

"I wonder who in the hell was in that car?"

Savannah

"I don't care, just as long we all are alright." Savannah replied.

They arrived at Shanna's place around four-thirty in the morning; after they made a quick stop at the Maryland Baptist Orphanage in Baltimore City, to drop off that duffle bag of money, courteously of Mr. Peewee's illegal activities. Peewee had already been stripped down and taped tightly to a metal chair; that had a hole cut out, so he can piss and shit in a can with a trash can liner filled with water and pine sol. Savannah checked him personally to make sure he couldn't get loose; be she and her crew went upstairs for some needed rest.

*****

Around seven in the morning, Shanna shook Savannah, waking her up; letting her know her mother was on the phone.

"Is everything alright Savannah? I tried calling you several times on your cell but it went straight into voice mail."

"I'm fine mama. I just turned my phone off, so I could get some rest. How are you, dad and the boys' doing?"

"They're fine. They're with your father out fishing. They are having so much fun, with so many daily activities, it's ridiculous. So you don't have to worry about them." She chuckled.

"I know you told me he's out with Devin and Chance, but how is daddy really doing, mama?"

"He's okay baby. He's doing just fine. Your father is tougher than you think."

"That's good."

"When are you going to stop by?"

"I'm not sure mama; I'll call, before I just pop up."

"Alright then, just be careful."

"I will ma. Love you."

"Love you too baby…bye." Savannah felt relieved the boys were having a great time and enjoying their summer and her mom and dad were alright. She laid her head back on the pillow and instantly fell back to sleep. It was almost eleven o'clock when she got up for good. She made her way to the kitchen.

"How did you sleep?" Shanna asked.

"Good." Savannah replied, rubbing her eyes.

"What do you want to eat?" Desha asked.

"I don't want any breakfast, just some coffee." After thirty minutes the ladies made their way to the basement to extract any information they could from Peewee. The basement floor was covered with plastic and placed Peewee still sitting in the chair, on top of a four inch by three feet piece of wooden board. Scented candles and those pine tree air fresheners that you put in your car, where throughout the basement. Savannah removed the tape from his mouth.

"Can you get me some water? I'm thirsty." Peewee asked licking his lips.

"Did you think about that, when one of your boys hit my girl in the jaw?" Savannah replied in a soft tone.

"Come on, I need something to drink; anything cold."

"Did you think about that when you wanted to rape us?"

"It was all a misunderstanding Savannah. I just need a cup of water. Please!" Shanna went upstairs and returned shortly with a glass of ice water. She walked over to Peewee. He began to lick his lips in anticipation of receiving some water. Shanna pulled up a chair directly in front of Peewee and began drinking the cold water in his face. "Did you really think I was going to give you something to drink?" Shanna said to Peewee as she stood up and walked away. He just looked at the four women with desperation, written all over his face. Savannah asked Desha to hand her the black bag, before kneeling down in front of him. "I have a cousin in the CIA, and he taught me some techniques on how to extract information from people, that I consider a threat to my well being. I'm going to ask you a few questions and if you don't give me the desired answers that I want to hear, then I will start placing these knives in parts of your body; that will cause you significant pain. Tynesha took position behind Peewee with an oversize thick cotton glove; while the others watch on.

"Why did you have people come after my father?"

"I came after your father, to lure you back." Peewee replied, singing like a bird, early in the morning.

Savannah

"Why?"

"We knew you had moved out of town, but didn't know where."

"Why did you want to know where I was?"

"Revenge for what you did to Ricky." Savannah couldn't believe what she was hearing, but wasn't really surprise. Tynesha lifted Peewees' chin and said.

"It's been five years since Ricky went to jail. Did you know what that mother fucker did to her?" Peewee just looked at her, without saying a word. "Well bitch, I asked you a question."

"Yeah, I knew."

"And still you have the audacity to come after my girl and her family?"

"That's bull shit." Desha added from the back of the room. Rage filled Savannah's body to the point, she lost her composer and slap Peewee in the mouth so hard, she split his top and bottom lip. Then she said aloud.

"I was minding my business, living my life and enjoying my family; when your boy disrupted my world and that disruption killed my husband and did a number on me." Tears now flowing from Savannah's eyes, she continued. "I can't have any more children. I have one kidney and assortment of other fucked up shit going on with me. So, you're looking at a bitch who don't give a fuck anymore." Shanna stood beside Savannah and placed her arm around her shoulders. In the mist of her anger she heard Tynesha cell vibrating. From what Savannah gathering, the call was unpleasant. "Savannah you need to take this call," Tynesha said with concern. When Savannah took the phone from her, Shanna walked over to Peewee and started throwing punches at his face as if was a punching bag. Desha jumped up and grabbed Shanna around both arms and pulled her away and scolded. "What's wrong with you girl? We suppose to be extracting information from him, not trying to kill him, at least not yet."

The call was from Valerie. What she said to Savannah buckled her knees, causing her to fall to the floor. Savannah's children have been kidnapped.

CHAPTER EIGHTTEEN
"How in the hell did you get in here?"

Savannah had a brief layover in Denver, before boarding a flight to Pueblo. The plane landed around 11a.m. local time, and she was so glad to get off that long flight. Some African guy around twenty-five, that was sitting next to her, was trying to pick her up the whole flight. Savannah tried to be nice to the young man, but he couldn't take a hint that she was not interested in him the least bit; so she had to hurt his feelings while shutting him down harshly. Once in the terminal, she began to thread her way through the many travelers; going to and from wherever. She made her way outside the terminal and boarded a shuttle for a short but relaxing ride to the Hertz rental office.

After reservation verification and what credit card she wanted the bill charged against, she was on her way to pick up a Chrysler 300. She threw her Dooney and Burke overnight bag on the passenger seat, started up the car, and turned on the radio to 89.3. 'Quiet Eyes' by Brandon Fields was playing. She took a deep breath and said a quick prayer before starting out on the twenty-nine mile drive to Florence. Driving along US 50, Savannah was taking in the beautiful sights. *It's something how a few hours ago, the scenery was green and vibrant on the east coast, now replaced by brownish and mountain terrain, on the west,* she thought to herself, as she drove down the road. Her mind began to drift, as she began to question herself on why she even took this trip. The trip was to see the man who had ruined her life and is in the process of trying to do it again. Thirty-five minutes later she pulled up in the parking lot of the prison. Savannah was taken back on how huge the facility was. She figured that's why they call this place "Supermax".

Savannah

After being thoroughly searched and escorted through a few metal security doors, she made her way into the visitation area. The visiting area looked like a cafeteria that could have been in any school in America; minus the food line. A few minutes later Ricky walked in wearing his prison best. He didn't look as handsome as she once remembered. The look on his face when he saw her was a mixture of surprise and anger.

As he sat down in front of her, he said. "How in the hell did you get in here? I know you're not on the list I provided to the prison staff. Are you Five-O or something?"

"No! I'm not Five-O, but if you keep fuckin' with me, you're gonna wish I was. Look, I didn't come here for a social visit. I came here to ask you, where are my children? They've been taken by someone you paid to do the deed. I want to know who has them, and I want to know now!" He just sat there and steered at her for a few second. "Bitch, are you crazy? You cut my shit off and sent me to this hell hole, for the next twenty years of my life. For however long I'm in here you are going to pay." Raising her voice, she replied.

"I'm going to pay? Did you forget how vicious I can be? I'm trying my best not go there. From one parent to another, I need you to call off your dogs and return my children back to me." A Native American correctional officer that was watching them walked over to the table and asked, "Ma'am is everything alright?" Savannah put her hand up indicating, everything was cool. The officer turned away and took up position back at the door.

"You started this shit! So do you really want to go to war with me? I advise you to pick and chose, who you fuck with Mr. Ricky Fontayne."

"Bitch, do you think you can put fear in my heart; because you know I have a family?"

"I'm not here to put fear in your heart. I'm here to find out who has my children." After her plea to Ricky, he smiled at her, and replied.

"Those are the casualties of war baby."

"So be it! I will pay a visit to your ex wife and daughter and put them to sleep. The money that is on your commissary will be transferred to someone else's account. Try me!"

"Bitch I will have you killed the minute you step foot back into DC." Savannah stood up and leaned toward him.

"Like you said, that's the casualty of war baby." She noticed a few inmates checking them out, so she took it to the next level. Standing erect, Savannah spoke loud enough for everyone to hear. "He's a K-9!" Simultaneously all the inmates in the visitation area, turned around in their direction. The term K-9 means snitch in prison language. Ricky nervously looked around and replied in a low voice.

"Keep fuckin' with me bitch and I will reach across this table and strangle the shit out of you. By the time the guards react I will have taken the life out of your body." Savannah gave him a smirk, not worrying about his comment and reached into her jacket pocket and retrieved a news article from the Washington Post. She then slid the article toward Ricky. In bold letters the headline read: **Inmate Stabbed To Death in one of Maryland's Correctional Institutes.** The article went on to read:

Washington, D.C. Aug 18 (UPI)—Warden Sheets of the federal Correctional Institute in Cumberland County, Maryland said Monday, he believe overcrowding may have contribute to the murder of an inmate in his cellblock Saturday night.

Maurice Fontayne, 24, a convicted drug kingpin from South East Washington, D.C. that was serving a life sentence, was found dead with thirty-six stab wounds to his upper torso. Ricky couldn't finish reading the article. He looked like he wanted to cry and seemed lost at the same time. Savannah stood up and said. "Those are the casualties of war baby."

"Bitch, I'm going to kill you; if it's the last thing I do." Rickey jumped up screaming, reaching for her neck with both hands. The guards came running over to restrain him.

Savannah

"Yeah, just like your brother." Savannah said with a smile, knowing it will irritate him like no one's business. Ricky continued to curse her while the guards took him away kicking and screaming.

"He's a K-9, you all better watch out." Savannah blurted out to the inmates, in the visiting area; knowing the word would spread amongst them like a California wild fire. Savannah continued to yell out, even though Ricky was no longer in the area. "When you screw over someone that was minding their business and undeserving of that other person's malice; stand by for the back lash."

Savannah's friend Andrew made some changes in the computer and by the time she reached the parking lot, Ricky had no money on his account, and any future funds would be diverted to other inmate's account. As she drove to the hotel, she called Shanna.

"I just finished having a conversation with Ricky. Nothing was productive."

"So what's next?"

"We need to prepare for war."

"You haven't said anything but a word cousin. If he really wants to go there, then we will go there."

"Shanna, I can call Val and get those guys that helped us out before." Savannah replied with uncertainty.

"Look cousin, you can call Val, if you really need to, but I believe we can handle this mother fucker and his crew; ourselves. Did you forget that we are highly train as well?"

"We'll talk more when I get back Shanna." Savannah pressed the button on her phone disconnecting the call, with thought's she didn't want to think about.

CHAPTER NINETEEN
"I'm out of feet Peewee"

When Savannah arrived at Thurgood Marshall Airport in Baltimore; Desha was there to greet her. "Your mom is a wreck, and your father is taking it hard. Tynesha and I are taking turns spending time with them."
"Where's Shanna?"
"She's gathering intelligence and weapons."
"My parents have been through a lot in the past five years. What pissed me off is, they should not be going through this nonsense. Meaning my close to death experience, Marcus's murder, my father getting a beat down outside his home along with my mother being shoved to the ground beside him, now my sons their grand children, are kidnapped. I'm sick and tired of being sick and tired. All those involved in disrupting my family's life will know who Savannah is, before they leave this life." Shanna pulled up behind them just as they stopped in front of her house. Savannah exited the car and the three had a quick chat, before Desha drove off; heading back to Savannah's parents' house. As she and Shanna walked toward the front door, Shanna informed her they've been feeding Peewee bread and water; just enough food to sustain him, to extract information. They took off their shoes in the foyer and headed for the basement.

They donned white hazmat suites that was at the bottom of the basement steps to deal with Mr. Peewee, he was about to feel a pissed off woman's rage. Savannah slapped him on the head a couple times with the handle of a knife; waking him up. He slowly opened his eyes and immediately began talking.
"You bitches, you mother fuckin' bitches." Savannah slapped him across his mouth.

Savannah

"You're not going to be calling us too many more bitches." He just looked at her with menacing eyes and blurted out.

"Fuck you!" Savannah kneeled down in front of him, and slammed a knife through his right foot. He screamed out in pain. When the pain subsided a little, Savannah spoke to him.

"I'm back from visiting Ricky. Now I want to hear what you have to say about the kidnapping."

"I stink, I have shit and piss on me and a knife through my foot. I need a shower and medical attention. Come on, let me take a shower." He said in a slurred voice.

"I don't give a damn about you stinking and wanting to take a shower. I have no sympathy for your pathetic ass. All I want from you is information on the whereabouts of my sons and if you don't give me what I want, you are going to start singing to the pied piper. Now where are my children?" Savannah asked in an elevated voice.

"I don't know." Shanna tears off a piece of duct tape and placed it over his mouth. "That's the wrong answer." Savannah said as she freed the knife from his foot and slammed it down through the left foot. He screamed in pain, but the sound was muffled by the tape over his mouth.

"I'm going to ask you again. Where are my children?" She rips the tape from his mouth.

"I told you, I don't know!" He replied, as slob streamed out his mouth.

"Well I don't believe you." Savannah responded as she wiggled the knife she had put through his left foot. Veins surfaced to his forehead and neck as he screamed and a flood of tears rolled down his cheeks. He struggled and squirmed fiercely in the chair, but to no avail.

"I'm out of feet Peewee. You better start telling me something. My children are scared and are somewhere they don't want to be." He didn't answer. Savannah then stuck the knife through his right leg just above the knee. He violently jerked his head back, catching Shanna off guard, hitting her in the chest knocking her back a few steps.

Spit and snot flew everywhere as Peewee screamed from the excruciating pain that consumed his body. Savannah gave him a few minutes for the pain to subside while retrieving another knife. Blood streamed from his wounds, down his limbs and onto the plastic beneath him. Grimacing from the pain, slurring some of his words and sounding out of breath, he managed to say. "It wasn't me or Ricky who sanctioned the kidnapping."

"Tell me something of importance Peewee!"

"Alright! alright!" Peewee responded as he was going in and out of consciousness.

"Stay with me Peewee, I don't have all day. I SAID I DON'T HAVE ALL DAY!" Savannah lost it for a second as she hammered another knife into the other leg. His eyes opened wide then closed tightly as he screamed in agony, but the volume wasn't as loud because Shanna had her hand over his mouth this time. When Peewee settled down, Shanna removed her hand.

"It's Karyn! She's behind all this man." Savannah looked at Shanna and Shanna looked at Savannah.

"What's the number?" She asked, checking if it's the same number she had called earlier. He rambled off seven digits and the number wasn't the same. "I know you're lying to me." In between asking God to help him and pleading for her mercy, he pleaded.

"I'm not lying. This is a good number for her." Shanna unzipped her suit and retrieved her throw-away-phone and dialed the number. Shanna tossed the phone over to Savannah.

"Hello!" A woman voice answered. It sounded like Karyn, but Savannah wasn't too sure; so she asked.

"Is this Karyn?"

"Who wants to know?" The woman responded with an attitude.

"Look I don't have time for this today. Ricky wants to know did you snatch Savannah's kids yet?"

"Yeah! About two day ago." Savannah moved slightly away from the receiver and acted like she was passing on the information; to someone else.

Savannah

"Let Ricky know she already got the kids." Placing the receiver back to her mouth, she continued. "Did you hear anything about Savannah looking for them?"

"Yeah, but she won't find them I have them stashed away in the projects, in South East D.C."

"Cool, I'll pass the word to Ricky."

"Who's this again?" Karyn asked. Savannah disconnected the call, without responding to her question. She looked at Shanna and Shanna knew Savannah was pissed at the highest level.

"Karyn is behind the kidnapping. My babies are in some damn projects in South East DC. We need to get to her house in a hurry, before she puts one and one together." Savannah stood up and came across Peewee's throat with a clean cut on his jugular. Blood flew everywhere.

"Damn Savannah! Can you give a sistah a warning next time?" She didn't answer her. She just pulled out her cell and called Tynesha.

"Hello."

"Tee, I need for you and Desha to pay Karyn a visit at her house. That bitch was behind the kidnapping all along. We'll catch up with you there in about an hour and a half."

"Do you want us to sit on the house or check to see if she's there?"

"Check her!"

"Okay, we're on our way. Bye." Savannah and Shanna dismembered Peewee's body, just like he did to so many people. They tripled bagged the body parts along with other kitchen trash, and some saw dust to soak up the blood. And quickly cleaned themselves up, and went to the Charles County dump, to get rid of the bags.

"Shanna, I'm really going to bring pain to that bitch."

"I feel you cuz."

"So will she!"

CHAPTER TWENTY
"An eye for an eye"

"Hello, is this Karyn?"

"Yes."

"My name is Tynesha. I'm one of Savannah's friends."

"So!"

"So, I'll be there shortly to put my foot in your ass. You're walking around like Ms. Innocent, when all along you had something to do with the kidnapping."

"Look, Savannah's friend, I don't give a shit about you coming over here. I don't give a shit about Savannah trying to locate her kids nor am I worried about if she ever sees those little fuckers again. Savannah was fucking my man before cutting his dick off and sending him to prison. She must pay for that shit." In a low whisper, Desha mouthed to Tynesha in a whisper tone, to keep her on the phone; that way they'll know she's at home when they arrive.

"Bitch, are you really that stupid? I know you didn't forget that Ricky was the one that sent those hit men to kill a federal judge, but ended up at the wrong house and killed her husband, not to mention almost killing her as well. She didn't ask for none of this. An eye for an eye, since her life was destroyed, she did the same to the man who was behind it. At least she dealt with him and didn't go after anyone in his family. Now you all are gunning for her, because you think she's wrong for what she did to and with Ricky. Now you tell me Karyn, you really don't see who's in the wrong here?"

"Well, I have the ball. I'm making the rules and I'm going to play the game the way I want to play it. Do you understand?" Karyn snapped.

"Is that right?"

"Yeah, that's right! So bitch, if you're coming, come on. I'll be here." On that note Karyn hung up the phone. Tee glanced at Desha and said, "Do you believe that bitch? She has the nerve to

Savannah

think Savannah started this mess. Then the bitch had the nerve to hang up on me."

"Tee, don't worry about it. You know we're on our way to her house to fuck her up. So fuck it, don't worry about it.

"I guess you're right. Did you know you use the word "fuck" a lot?"

"What does that have to do with the mission at hand?"

"I just thought, your kitty is crying for attention, so the word fuck is heavily on your mind."

"Girl as soon as I get back to my man, I'm going to get my kitty taken care of," Desha responded, swirling her hips.
"I don't know what I'm going to do with you." They both chuckled as they continued driving toward Karyn's house.

*****

Shortly after hanging up the phone, Karyn's doorbell rang. She answered the door with a P7M13 9MM with a 13 round metal magazine inserted by her hand, by her side.
"You finally made it. I like people who keep their word. Don't just stand there come inside. Savannah and her bitches are on their way over here." Karyn said as she turned around and started to walk back through the foyer. Suddenly there was a loud thud and Karyn fell to the floor. She was knocked out. She never saw the blow coming.

"This is a nice gun. Let's get her upstairs and take her clothes off. Then we'll put her ass in the bath tub." Karyn was dragged upstairs to her master suite and had her clothes removed before being dragged to the bathroom and placed in her tub.

"Break one of those ammonia capsules and wake this bitch up." One of the assailants said to the other. Karyn slowly began to awaken only to find herself naked and bound in the bathtub.

"What the fuck is this shit?" Karyn asked defiantly.

"Well, I want some information and if you don't give me what I want, when I'm finish with you, you will give me names of every missing child from here to California. Now where do you have those boy's stashed?"

"You betray me for Savannah?"

"Who said, I'm doing this for Savannah?"

"Bitch, I aint telling you sh…!" Before Karyn could complete her sentence, her hoop earrings were ripped from her earlobe.

"Ahhh, shit!" Karyn cursed from the seething pain.

"Tell me what I want to know, and I'll be easy on you."

"I like it rough."

"Oh, you're one of those gangster bitches trying to be tough. Put some duct tape over her mouth, and then slice off her nipples." Karyn tried to struggle, but it was fruitless due to her restraints. As the knife severed her left nipple from her breast, Karyn screamed in agony, but her cries were muffled by the tape. She then passed out. Karyn came to, blinking her eye, trying to focus, when the knife came across her right nipple severing it, Karyn jerked back hitting her head against the wall; knocking herself out.

"Wake up bitch, don't pass out on me again." An ammonia capsule was broken and waved under her nose. She wakes up after a few passes. "You wanted to be a gangster, now deal with the consequences. Since you didn't want to talk, I'm going to make sure we don't have that problem again. Pass me those pliers. I'm going to start by pulling this big toe nail off." Karyn muffled screams were so intense the tape that covered her mouth came loose. Snot, blood and sweat poured from Karyn's body.

"ALRIGHT!" Karyn yelled out.

"Now that you know, I'm not fuckin' around with you, are you ready to talk to me?" Seeing they meant business and barely able to talk, Karyn gave up the information.

"They're at the Mayfield apartments on Hayes Street, apartment C, in south east DC," she mumbled.

"I hope this is the truth. You better not be fuckin' with me."

"I'm not! That's the God honest truth. Please, I beg you, no more pain."

"Now why did you have to be such a hard ass? Slice that bitch's throat." Within seconds the tub was filled with blood as Karyn lay motionless, still breathing but dying slowly, from the wound to her throat.

Savannah

*****

Tee and Desha finally arrived at Karyn's place. Parking down the street, both women take a deep breath.

"Desha, are you ready to kick a little butt?"

"You know I am," Desha responded rubbing her hands together after putting lotion on them. They both exited the vehicle and walked toward the house. Desha kept an eye on the windows of the house, while Tynesha rang the doorbell. The women Glocks were on ready as they held them close to their sides, but not visible to neighbors or passer byres'. They began to check the exterior of the house. The doors were locked and as they peered through the windows, there wasn't any activities going on inside. They put their weapons away and went back to the vehicle and waited for Savannah and Shanna.

"I know that bitch is in the house. I just got off the phone with her," Tee said.

"Maybe she had the calls transferred to her cell or to another number." Desha enlightened Tee as she twist the cap on the green bottle of Mountain Dew.

CHAPTER TWENTY-ONE
"Damn! Someone beat us to the party"

Tynesha and Desha were sitting in a burgundy Navigator, down the street from Karyn's house when Savannah pulled up.
"Did you talk to Karyn?" Savannah asked.
"On the cell, but not in person, we knocked on the door, rang the bell and no one answered. We even looked through the windows to see if we could see any movement, nothing."
"Since we've been here, there's been no activity," Desha added as she took a sip of Mountain Dew.
"Well, let's go inside and pay that bitch a visit." Savannah said to them, before pulling off to park the car.
Savannah and Shanna took the front door, while Desha and Tynesha covered the back. Savannah rang the bell and waited a few minutes, while checking out the windows for any signs of movement. There was no answer. She rang it again, and still no answer. Savannah put on a pair of latex glove and pulled out a small leather pouch with an assortment of small tools and uses one to pick the lock. She signaled for the others to follow. There were no signs of anyone, as they split up and began to search the house.
It wasn't long before Tynesha yelled for everyone to come upstairs. When Savannah reached the top of the stairs, Tynesha was standing in the doorway of the bathroom with her gun at the ready.
"What's up Tee?" Savannah asked as she walked closer to her. Karyn was lying in the tub as if she was taking a bath. The problem was there was no water, she was unclothed and she was dead. Her blood traveled down the drain, like lava from a volcano. Despite the horror staring them in the face, Savannah checked her for any vital signs. There was none.
Savannah's mind was racing back and forth as she wondered who in the hell could have taken her out like that, as she stared at her lifeless body. It was apparent from the wounds inflicted on her

Savannah

body, that she was tortured. The bathroom was clean. There were no dirty towels, no blood spatter, nothing.

"Damn! Someone beat us to the party." Desha said as she checked the nearby rooms. Savannah looked at Tynesha for some kind of answer, but she assured her that no one had came or left the house since they arrived.

"How could this have happened? As soon as you got off the phone with Karyn, you called Tee and Desha," Shanna said out loud. "And we left the house before Tee got off the phone with you."

"We need to get the fuck up outta of here, just in case the police are on their way and someone is trying to set us up," Savannah suggested, as they hurriedly made their way to the front door.

"I hope we didn't drop any DNA around the house," Shanna said with a worried expression on her face.

"I hear you girl," Desha added.

"Did anybody see any signs of her daughter?" Savannah asked, as they walked to their vehicles.

"I didn't know she had one," Shanna replied as she pressed the button on her key chain to unlock the vehicle doors. Savannah still couldn't fathom what had happened and began feeling queasy as anxiety began to consume her. She had to take slow easy breaths. She kept thinking over and over, who could possibly have her children? What part of South East were they in? How are they being treated? Are they being abused? She knew she had to composure herself. Moreover, she had to remain strong for the team, the mission and most of all her sons.

Later that day, the women were at Savanna's parents' house. They were sitting in the kitchen having a bite to eat, while trying to figure out their next move; when Savannah's father called her to come upstairs. She walked passed her mother who was asleep on the couch, and then paused for a minute and placed an Angora over her; before continuing upstairs.

She walked into parent's bedroom. There her father sat in a wicker chair by the window. He had a look on his face that she had never saw before. It was a look of desperation, fear, anger and confusion. It frightened her. And Savannah wasn't the type to be easily frightened.

"Daddy, what's going on?" she asked as she sat beside him on the floor.

"I have had enough Savannah, people coming out of the wood works messing with my family. I said to you once before, that if anyone brings harm to that woman that I love, down stairs, God knows what I would do to them. I know what you did to Peewee. You took him out before I was well enough to do the deed. But you were late getting to Karyn," he said with a smile. She was in shock. She couldn't believe what her father was saying. *How did he know about Karyn? He couldn't have killed Karyn; and if he did, how did he get to her before Tee and Desha arrived at the house and leave without them seeing him? How did he know what I did to Peewee?* Savannah thought to herself. This wasn't the first time her father knew what she had done or what she had intentions of doing. This baffled Savannah as she sat there listening to him.

"Daddy did you kill Karyn?"

"They should have never taken my grand babies or put their hands on your mother." He then turned toward the window and became quiet. Savannah got up to walk away, when he reached for her wrist.

"They made a mistake picking our family to mess with, and it's a mistake they will pay for dearly. Don't worry about the police; you are untouchable because you are invisible." He released her wrist and closed his eyes as if he was going to sleep.

"Daddy!"

"I'm tired baby. Don't worry; we're going to have those babies back soon. Let me sleep honey." Savannah stood there looking at her father for a minute before walking away confused as ever.

Did he really kill Karyn? What did he mean I was invisible? She thought to herself. *I wonder if his Viet Nam days are catching up to him.* Her father served in the Special Forces where he was involved in a lot of secret missions that involved killing the enemy up close and personal. He never told her about his exploits, but her mother did. Valerie had also informed Savannah that her father was

Savannah

still on the Central Intelligent Agency payroll. Additionally, the CIA would call him from time to time for advice on certain top-secret missions. Yet Savannah never really put any thought into it; until now. When she got downstairs, her mother was no longer on the couch. Tynesha was sitting there watching reruns of Law and Order.

"Where's my mother?"

"She wanted to go to Wal-Mart, so Shanna took her." Desha said, reaching for a bottle of water in the refrigerator.

"Let me ask you something."

"What?"

"Did anyone tell my father what we did to Peewee?"

"What you mean?" Tynesha asked.

"My father knew what went down with Peewee and Karyn."

"You got to be kidding," Desha said almost choking from a swig of water she had just taken.

"It shouldn't be a question about any of us talking. You know none of us roll that way."

"I know, but I had to ask anyway."

CHAPTER TWENTY TWO
"The apartment was a blaze"

Nine o'clock the next night, the women was on the I-295 north heading toward Nanni Burroughs road. Savannahs mind was focused on the Mayfield apartments on Hayes Street, where her sons were being held. Thirty minutes later, they arrived at their designated location. Savannah parked across the street from the location they were given. Desha got out the car and took a position on an adjacent building rooftop, across the street from the targeted building.

Shanna entered the building to verify the apartment number. Everyone was wearing their earpiece and they stayed in constant communication with one another while the mission unfolded. Savannah was anxious knowing her sons were less than fifty yards away, but it seemed like they were miles away. The situation was deadly and delicate all at the same time. They were going into a confined area to eliminate a threat, and had to stay mindful that bullets can go through the walls into other apartments. Not to mention they had to save two precious packages at the same time.

"Ladies, check." Savannah spoke into the mouthpiece checking everyone's signal.

"I hear you loud and clear on the roof top," Desha replied. Her job was to cover any outside threats with a suppressor attached to a high-powered sniper rifle.

"I'm up on the inside," Shanna blared out. Her job along with Tynesha was to eliminate any threats on the inside, while Savannah grabbed the precious packages.

"Okay, ladies, let's do this," Savannah said as she and Tynesha exited the SUV. The women were about thirty feet from the building when an explosion went off in the intended apartment knocking Savannah and Tynesha to the ground.

Savannah

They were dazed and confused. Savannah got to her feet and began running towards the building screaming for her children. Tynesha caught up with her as they entered the building. The place was billowing with choking black smoke. The apartment was a blaze, but that didn't stop Savannah from trying to enter. Tynesha grabbed her and held her back.

"There's nothing we can do. Let's go before the police arrive," Tynesha said to her in a comforting voice. Savannah could hardly walk thinking about her children.

"Where is, Shanna?" she asked. She was nowhere to be found. "Oh, my God, she must have been killed in the explosion, with my babies."

"Let's get out of here!" Tynesha barked as she held on to Savannah, as they staggered away from the building. It was chaotic as people were running into the building to assist those that were hurt. In the same breath people were running from the building with pain and horror etched on their faces.

Desha had broken her rifle down and made her way over to Savannah and Tynesha. Once they were inside the SUV, Savannah began to cry uncontrollably. She called out for her sons and Shanna. She was in panic mode. Her cell phone was vibrating, but she was so distraught she turned a deaf ear to it. It was Desha who answered the phone. The call seemed to last for only a minute, she had a bewildered look on her face.

"Savannah, some chick said your boys were not in the apartment. They were moved to a house in Fort Washington."

"Moved? Who are they?" Savannah asked. Desha looked at the caller ID.

"There's no data," She responded. "The caller said she would call back with the updated information. But she did say the kids had been moved there twenty-four hours ago and the explosion at the apartment was to leave no witnesses."

"Whoever that bitch was on the phone killed my cousin." Savannah screamed, as the tears mixed with the black smut ran down her face.

"There she is!" Tynesha yelled out. Shanna was walking towards the SUV with a slight limp. Savannah jumped out and ran over to help her back to the vehicle.

"We thought you were killed," Savannah said aloud with a concerned and relieve look on her face; as she hugged her cousin for dear life.

"I would have been, if you didn't tell me to go check the window outside." Shanna said.

"I didn't tell you to check on any windows." Savannah said, with raised eyebrows, as she looked at Tynesha and Desha.

"Well, someone did. Y'all didn't hear it on your ear piece?"

"Nah, none of us heard that." Desha told her.

"I'm sorry Savannah about Devin and Chance, someone have to pay for that. I will make that a priority in my life," Shanna said with tear filled eyes.

"They're not dead baby." Savannah informed her. Shanna could only stare at the others, with her mouth slightly open.

"Well somebody, tell me something!" Shanna demanded still looking in their faces.

"All we know is after the explosion some female had called my cell and told me the kids had been moved the day before to a location in Fort Washington. She will give me a call later with the updated information, on the whereabouts of my sons." Savannah briefed her.

"How did this person get your cell number?" Shanna asked.

"I don't have a clue." The area was now flooded with firefighters, police, and spectators.

"Let's get the hell outta here and regroup at my house," Shanna suggested, as Desha jumped in the driver's seat and they pulled away; leaving the chaotic scene behind them.

CHAPTER TWENTY THREE
"Were you apart of that?"

The women cleaned up their wounds, took showers and poured themselves a drink. They gathered in the family room to discuss what had happened earlier. One of the first things they discussed was the phone call Desha took on Savannah's cell. They were all wondering how the person knew so much information about Savannah's children, and their relocation and the explosion. Did they watch the whole scene unfold? These were questions of concern, but the awaiting phone call and the location of Savannah's children were of top priority. While the women chatted, Savannah was giving instructions and getting an equipment check from them, when her cell rang. She thought it was the anonymous caller and so did everyone else. But it wasn't, it was her friend Valerie.

"I heard what went down last night, on the news. Were you part of that?"

"Yeah, but we didn't set off that explosion."

"Did you take any casualties?"

"No, but we had a close call though."

"Good. As long as everyone is all right, that's what counts. I have something to share with you. Do you have a minute?"

"Sure."

"Your mother heard your plans about what you and your girls were going to do in South East."

"Damn!" Savannah said out loud, holding her forehead.

"Your mother use to work for the Central Intelligence Agency, just like your father. Your mother was held in high regards, because she was one on the best agents that came through their doors. Technically she was more dangerous than your father."

"What?"

Savannah

"That's why you are as good as you are, it must be in the genes."

"I can't believe what you are telling me."

"Believe it honey. The only reason I'm telling you this, is because you don't have to worry about the police. Besides reuniting with your talented team, your mother still has major connections and will use them when it comes to protecting her family."

"Does my father know that my mother work for the agency?"

"That's where they met honey."

"Valerie, you know you are blowing my mind."

"I'd rather blow your mind than to see you get blown up. Your mother and father aren't as frail as you may think they are."

I guess that's what they meant by saying I was invisible, Savannah thought to herself. Valerie continued, "They called in some markers and everything is cool. Now that you're back in town the already high unsolved homicides are getting higher."

"I didn't ask anyone to take my children and mess with my mother and father."

"Believe me baby girl, they had the situation covered. Five years ago, when you were on your spree, your father had your back covered the whole time. Do you remember when you called me, when you felt something wasn't right on your parents block a couple of weeks ago?"

"Yeah."

"Well, I called your mother and she made a call. That's why those gentlemen showed up, not because of me."

"But they said you sent them."

"I was the middle person. We are not trying to deceive you, but we can't make what we do public knowledge."

"I appreciate what they have done, especially now that I know about their expertise, but I don't want them to be involved in what is going down any more."

"I wasn't going to tell you, but I talked to your parents just before calling you. I told them to stand down and let you handle your business. They agreed reluctantly, so do what you have to do baby. This is your fight, so handle your business.

I'll call you in a few days, oh, yeah, before I get off, I want to let you know, you have a guardian angel by your side."

"Who is this guardian . . . ?" Before Savannah could finish her sentence the call went dead. She wanted to know what guardian angel Valerie was talking about.

Savannah informed the girls on what she and Valerie talked about, except for the part about her parents being in the C.I.A. She just didn't feel like explaining her parent's lives at the time. Savannah was very weary, and was about to called it a day, and get some needed rest. Shanna's wanted to spend time with her man, after what she had just been through. She put together an overnight bag and was heading over to her boyfriend's house. She said her kitty was purring and needed some milk, because it was hungry. Savannah managed to laugh at what her cousin said. She loved her cousin dearly, and wanted the best for her. Sounding like two kids, Desha and Tee said it wasn't fair Shanna was getting her kitty cared for and theirs were starving just as much. Shanna told them she had some toys upstairs, and they could help themselves to them, but they have to clean them off with alcohol and bleach when they are done with them.

"Fuck you!" Desha replied jokingly with her hands on her hips.

"Bitch!" Tee yelled out.

Shanna laughed, and before walking out the door said, "I'll be a happy bitch getting fuuuucked all night. She looked at Savannah and put her hand up to her ear as if to say call me if anything comes up. Savannah nodded in acknowledgement. Savannah had some empathy for Desha and Tee, her own kitty needed a meal, but she had to put that thought to the side for now because her sons were still out there somewhere and getting them back was much more important than any dick or toy.

Savannah finally cuddled up in bed with the current issue of Essence Magazine. As she flipped through the pages, she came across a poem titled: **SAVED** by Elizabeth

Savannah

Pain, anger, agony, these are the things that can get the best of me. Always messing me up, making my body corrupt. I can't take it anymore.

Now I'm down on the floor with my hands lifted up and my voice raised up high. I'm finally giving up because you are in control.

I'm willing to go and take a stand.
I'm willing to go and change my ways.

My salvation, I'm willing to claim, here are my sorrows, and here is my pain. Now that you hear me Lord, I just want to say thank you.

Thank you Lord, for your sacrifices of my sins,
Thank you Lord, for forgiveness of my sins,
Thank you Lord, for saving me from my sins,

I'm finally saved.
Yes Lord, I'm finally saved.

The more Savannah thought about the poem, the more she felt it was written for her. As sleep overtook her body and mind, she placed the magazine by her side and dozed off.
It was around two in the morning, when she was awakened by Robin Thicke's 'Lost Without U' ring tone.
"Hello," she answered, still half asleep.
    The woman's voice on the other end of the line said, "Your sons are being held in Fort Washington, in a subdivision called Tantallon Preserve. The address is 12247 Diggs Terrace." Savannah was wide awake now and scrambled for a pen and paper to write down the information.
    "There's no need to write any of this down, if you're looking for a pen. There's a blue print of the house and location in an envelope at your front door." Savannah tried to ask a few more questions, but the line went dead. Grabbing her gun, she immediately went down stairs and cautiously opened the front door.

Brooklen Borne

An eight by eleven tan envelope was stuck in the screen door. She looked around, but couldn't see anything, it was pitch black outside. She called Shanna and awoke the others. A half hour later, they all gathered at the kitchen table. Tynesha turned on the coffee maker. Desha was doing an equipment check, and Savannah was filling them in on the call. Shanna arrived twenty minutes later. Savannah opened the envelope and they began to look over the contents. The house was a colonial style four bedroom, three and a half bath, with a completed basement. The bedrooms were upstairs and her sons were being held in the basement area. The instructions continued to read: *Most important, everyone in the house is the enemy; do not hesitate to kill. If you hesitate, they will kill you.* It was signed Nevaeh, Your Guardian Angel. Everything was laid out on a platter for them. Savannah passed the papers around for everyone to examine.

"Who is Nevaeh?" Shanna asked.

"I guess she's our guardian angel." Tynesha added.

Savannah looked at the letter and the diagram and replied, "I guess you're right." Desha looked at the paper, then at the name and said, "Nevaeh spelled backward is Heaven; I hope she's not that crazy bitch from that old Monique's reality T.V. show, Flavor of Love Charm School; that use to come on." Everyone laughed except for Savannah.

"I hope she's not either," Savannah added. An eerie feeling came over her, it was scary, but she had to put it on the back burner and gear up to get her children back.

An hour later, the women were packed and heading to the address that was given. As they drove on 95/495 south, Savannah threw in the CD "The Big Pay Back" by James Brown. They all began grooving to the funky lyrics. How appropriate was that?

They arrived around four o'clock, and parked down the block. It was a full moon and a slight breeze was blowing, a perfect night for their mission. They wore black clothes, with lightweight boots. They were dressed like any S.W.A.T. team across the nation, ski masks and all.

Savannah gathered everyone around the car to give last minute instructions. "Ladies this is it. Everyone check your gear and make

Savannah

sure you are wearing your vest. Let's get through this without the loss of life, but keep in mind if they engage, they die. Shanna, take out the security system. Tee, position yourself whereas to give us maximum cover. Desha set the implosion devices throughout the basement, while I get my babies. Are there any questions?" Everyone shook their heads no. "Okay, from here on out arm and hand signals. Let's do this."

CHAPTER TWENTY FOUR
"A gun battle ensued."

    The women made their way to the perimeter of the house. Shanna disabled the security system. Savannah cut out a big square piece of glass from the sliding glass window and waited a few minutes to see if there was a dog on the premises. Seeing there wasn't one, they made entry. Desha and Savannah made their way to the basement door. Savannah slowly opened it and there were three huge men playing cards.
Savannah didn't see any signs of Devin or Chance. She signaled to Desha, that three guys were just beyond the door. She moved in front of Savannah. Savannah pushed the door opened and thump, thump, thump. Desha had taken the men out, with shots to the head. Savannah made her way to the north east section of the basement, where her children were being held.
Devin and Chance were asleep. Savannah shook them gently so not to scare them. When they opened their eyes and recognized the woman in front of them was their mother, they jumped into her arms; giving her an abundance of tight hugs and kisses. Savannah covered their mouths to keep them from screaming mommy.
    "Shhh," she whispered. "Mommy's here to take you home. You have to stay quiet, okay."
They both whispered back, "Okay, mommy."
Desha had set the devises throughout the basement and signaled for the other's to come down. It would be easier to leave the house from the basement walkout. This was easier than they thought, until a woman came out the bathroom, fixing her pants and yelled out. "What the hell is going on?" A gun battle ensued. Shanna went down. Savannah motioned to Tee to take the boys to the car, while she and Desha laid cover fire.

Savannah

"Shanna, Shanna!" Savannah yelled, reloading a clip and placing it in her glock. She glanced back and saw Shanna rolling around on the floor. She and Desha made their way to the top of the stairs, shooting at anything that was in front of them. Savannah told Desha to get Shanna and get the hell out of there. She quickly went throughout the house, checking to see if there were any other children there. There were none.

Savannah was now taking on fire from at least four people. She set off a few smoke grenades near the stairs leading to the basement. The basement area began to fill with thick gray smoke. As she exited the house, Desha set off the imploding devices. After a several flashes, the house began to collapse inward; everything came straight to the ground, without much noise. If anyone was still alive in the house, they would not be walking out.

Savannah continued running back toward the team. She was halfway in the car when Tee began pulling away. Half way up the block she turned on the headlights and they were gone. Savannah looked at Shanna and asked, if she was alright, Desha turned and said, "This girl got nine lives. She's fine."

Shanna told Savannah that she took one in the vest, and it felt like someone had hit her in the chest with a baseball bat and knocked the wind out of her.

"Thank God, you're alright," Savannah said as she hugged her two boys. She looked them over and asks them were they all right, and did anybody do anything to them. They both assured her, that nothing was wrong with them and they were all right.

"Thank goodness for whoever gave us the layout of the house, it helped us out big time," Savannah said to everyone.

"I agree with you on that." Tee said, with a grin. When they arrived back at Shanna's place, it was still dark. As they exited the car, Savannah saw two figures sitting on the steps. She told Devin and Chance to stay in the car, and gave Tee instructions that if any shooting begins to haul ass with her sons and take them to a safe place. Shanna and Savannah had enough space between them as they walked toward the house. As they got closer, Savannah quickly noticed it was two young women.

"Hello Savannah." One of the women greeted, as if she knew her for a long time.

"Who are you?" Savannah asked.

"I'm Karyn's step daughter." Savannah quickly aimed her gun at the woman's head, as Shanna did the same to the other woman. "I see everything went well." The woman continued to speak in a calm voice, never taking her eyes off Savannah.

"I'm going to ask you one time, and one time only, what is your business here?" Shanna asked.

"Relax. I'm on your side. My name is Nevaeh, and I'm the guardian angel." Shanna slowly lowered her gun, with a bewildered expression on her face.

"Why did you help us? What's in this for you?" Savannah asked, with some suspicion.

"I just wanted to make things right. What had been done to you and your family was wrong and it had to be stopped." Feeling some compassion, Savannah told Nevaeh, that she was sorry for the loss of her stepmother.

"Why? She was a major contributor in the kidnapping of your children. Yes, Peewee and Ricky were players in this revenge game, but when Peewee lied to her, telling her that you were fuckin' Ricky on a regular, she felt betrayed and went after your kids. She was easily influenced by anything Peewee said to her.

She knew there wasn't ever going to be a chance of spending the rest of her life with a man she was truly in love with. So she allowed herself to be manipulated and blamed you, even though she knew Ricky started this whole mess. Ricky, Peewee and everyone associated with getting at you were all no good criminals. The world is better off without those two." Without saying another word, Nevaeh got up and walked toward her silver Lexus. Just as she opened the door to get in, she turned around and said, "My girl and I did the deed to Karyn. Oh, one other thing, I kept your parent's informed on what was going on, that's how they knew your move. I'm very good at surveillance."

"Nevaeh?

"That's me."

Savannah

"Do well in college. You ain't the only one that had done her homework." Savannah smiled at her. Nevaeh then got in her Lexus and drove away into the night. As they watched her drive away, Savannah wondered how she dealt with the pain of not having a mother, father or even a step mother and did a quick prayer, hoping that she would find some peace within herself. Tee exited the car and opened the driver's side passenger door and Savannah's sons ran up to her, hugging her around her waist and thighs.

Unbeknownst to the ladies, two cars were parked on the opposite side of the street from Shanna's house. The vehicle parked directly in the middle of the block had four occupants inside. The other vehicle that was parked further down the street had two men inside. The men in both cars observed the conversation between Savannah and Nevaeh. One of the four occupants slowly moved the night vision binoculars from his eyes, and etched on his face was a look that could kill the most harden criminal.

"This is the disloyal shit I'm talking about. I don't care if you are right or wrong, when you are family or close enough friends to be called family; you stick together no matter what the situation." The man with the binoculars said aloud, not talking to anyone in particular.

"So what you think we should do?" One of the men asked.

"She has to be eliminated. In order for our organization to grow, we need to set the example like those before us. And it must be an example that will send a message to everyone in our line of business. They need to know that if you cross any of us, we will take your life with no questions ask. If I even think that someone crossed me, I will send them to heaven or hell, not giving a fuck where they end up, as long as they are no longer on this earth," the man with the binoculars replied, as the others listened.

As Nevaeh pulled away from the curb, the car with the four occupants followed behind. They trailed Nevaeh for a good ten minutes, before the other vehicle with the two occupants picked up the tail. Both vehicles switched off tailing the two ladies until they found out where their final destination was.

"I can't believe we're going to college in September," Nevaeh friend said with excitement, as she looked over at her.

"I know! I'm looking forward to getting away from all this mess. The street education has been great, but the streets aren't for me." Nevaeh replied, as she stared straight ahead as if she was in a trance.

"I'm with you on that statement. I hope Karyn's body don't come back to bite us in the ass, as we move forward."

"As long as we keep our mouth shut about it, we will be alright." Nevaeh replied looking her friend straight in the eyes.

"Come on, let's go inside and get some sleep. My boyfriend will be over to pick us up to register for classes in a few hours." Nevaeh just nodded her head in agreement before saying, "That sounds so good to me, because I'm tired as hell."

Just as the two started walking up the walkway to the front door, the car with the two occupants that was trailing them pulled up.

"Hello, beautiful ladies. How are you this morning?" The driver blurted out the window.

"We're doing fine, but we can't hold a conversation at this time," Nevaeh said to the men, before turning to her friend. "I don't believe these clowns think we want to hook up with them, besides the sun is not even up."

Before her friend could respond, the men alighted from the car after pulling over to the curb and approached the two women.

"Well, sweetheart, let me give you my card, so we can hook up at a later date."

Taken aback momentarily, Nevaeh responded, "No, I'm not interested."

"Oh, it's like that pretty lady?" Both women entered the house closing the door.

"I don't give up so easily," one of the men yelled, loud enough for Nevaeh to hear.

"I can't believe that guy tried to throw game on us so early in the morning," Nevaeh said annoyed to her friend.

"A hard dick, don't care what time it is." Her friend responded and both women laughed at the statement. Too tired to make it upstairs they sat on the couch, and within minutes they were fast asleep.

Savannah

*****

It was early afternoon and the women were still asleep, when they were awakened by rapid knocks on the door. With crinkled brows, both woman looked at each other as if to say who in the hell is that at the door? Nevaeh opened the door and couldn't believe her eyes. It was the same two guys from earlier in the morning.

"Hey pretty lady, I told you I wasn't going to give up. Here take my card and give me a call."

"I told you once before that I'm not interested."

"Come on now, just take the card."

"Okay, I'm going to take your card but leave me alone, because I'm tired. Do we understand each other?"

"Baby, I understand you loud and clear." The persistent guy replied. As Nevaeh reached to take the card, the guy pulled out a gun and forced her back inside the house. The second guy signaled for the vehicle with the four occupants inside. The men parked in front of the house. They got out and entered the house.

"Come on now, all this for a date? Shit, you must be desperate." Nevaeh responded, looking at the guy who pulled the gun. "Bitch, if you don't shut up and sit the fuck down, I'm gonna sit you down." Nevaeh and her friend sat down on the couch, as ordered.

"What is this all about?" Her friend asked.

"It's about betrayal." A commanding voice interjected,, indicating that he was in charge. As he approached the two ladies, he was followed by three other men carrying black duffle bags.

Nevaeh and her friend knew this was something serious and to make matters worse they had left their weapons in the car. The only other weapon they had a chance of getting to, was a shotgun, but it was upstairs in the bedroom. Nevaeh friend signaled to her with her eyes that she was going to make a run for it upstairs.

As she ran for the stairs, one of the men caught her in the back with a closed fist. It caused her to fall face first on the stairs landing as she writhed in pain. Nevaeh jumped up and slugged the guy in the mouth that hit her friend and took off up the stairs toward the bedroom.

The leader sat comfortably on the couch as one of his other men chased after Nevaeh and caught her at the top of the stairs. He grabbed her by her hair and pinned her against the wall; by her throat; just before he tossed her down the stairs. She screamed out in pain as her shoulder and hip hit the edge of each step. Hurt, dazed and barely able to move, Nevaeh tried to get up, but couldn't. He walked down to her taking her by the collar and slung her back into the living room. She landed face first onto the floor.

"Sit both these bitches in a chair and secure them." The leader commanded one of the men. Both women hands and feet were duct tape tightly to the chair, they were seated in. The leader pulled another chair around and sat down in front of them, looking at them intensely before asking, "Why would you betray Ricky, Maurice and Peewee?"

"What the fuck are you talking about? I didn't betray anybody." Nevaeh manage to say through the pain.

"Your Ricky's daughter and you two killed Karyn. Now that's some disloyal shit."

"I don't know what you are talking about.

"I'm going to ask you again and when I do, be careful how you answer me, because your friend comfort depends on you."

"Look man, like I said before, I don't know what you are talking about."

"Why do you have to tie us up to ask us questions, we don't know anything?" Nevaeh friend added.

The guy in charged glanced over to his associate closest to Nevaeh friend and with a closed fist the guy punched her in the mouth, splitting her lip and knocking a tooth out. Blood went everywhere.

"Look jackass! You don't have to do that," Nevaeh blurted out, almost in tears.

"You know what Nevaeh; I'm not going to play games with you.

"How do you know my name?" The leader put his hand out and one of his associates placed an envelope in it. He removed some pictures from it and tossed them onto her lap. The pictures were of her and Savannah having a conversation less than an hour ago.

Savannah

As she looked at the photos, Nevaeh was wondering, *how did they get these pictures of them, I just left Savannah not long ago. Shit! They were watching me all along.*

"Now, what I'm supposed to think when I see you talking to the chick that killed Peewee and sent Ricky to jail? What kind of conversation would you two might be having?" Nevaeh could only look at him as he continued. "Also, didn't you two bitches kill your step mom for Savannah?" Nevaeh still didn't say a word.

"If I don't get the answers that I want, I'm going to have my associate start cutting off parts of your friend limbs. You know the routine, starting with her fingers and working down to her toes. You get the picture." Nevaeh remained quiet. She knew her friends' boyfriend would soon be coming to the house, because he was already on his way back from New York, and she was trying to buy some time.

"Cover her mouth," The leader commanded, as Nevaeh looked at her friend's mouth being taped.
He stood in front of her friend and ripped open her blouse and cut away her bra exposing the woman's perfectly round breast. The woman's plea fell on death ears as her voice was muffled by the duct tape. He then opened the black duffle bag and retrieved a pair of grip pliers. Before Nevaeh could react, he had clamped down on her nipple and removed a straight razor from his front pant pocket and sliced off her right nipple. Her muffled scream was intense as pain, fear, death and blood consumed the young woman's body.

"Okay! I'll tell you what you want to know. Ask me anything, I'll tell you, just leave her alone," Nevaeh pleaded.
Nevaeh's request was ignored as the leader sling the severed nipple to the floor and clamp on to the left one and sliced that one off for good measure. The pain was too excruciating and the young woman passed out. Nevaeh was screaming, as she jumped around trying to free herself.

"Okay, I know Savannah and I know what she had done."
"So why did you side with her and not your father and Peewee?"
"I didn't side with her like you may think. I did Karyn, so this nonsense that clouded my life would stop."

Nevaeh sang as she looked over at her friend who was still passed out; with blood all over her. "Karyn had orchestrated the kidnapping of Savannah's children and as you know when you mess with a woman's kids, it's like you're taking meat from a pit bull and then teasing it. By her kidnapping those kids, you can expect some major shit to jump off."

"You don't have a clue, who the fuck I am? Do you!" The leader said with a disgusting expression on his face.
Nevaeh studied his face, for a few seconds before shaking her head no.

"It's obvious you lived a sheltered life and now you're trying to be hard." The leader then looked over to one of his associates and told him to wake the passed out woman with some smelling salt. The associate did as he was instructed. She woke up groggy, fighting off the smell of ammonia by shaking her head from side to side. Trying to regain her vision, as she looks around the room and still in a lot of pain, the woman began to cry out as the pain of her severed nipples took over her body. Nevaeh's face was soaked with tears, as she looked at her friend.

"Look, I will do anything. Just leave her alone," Nevaeh yelled out.

"Would you give up your life for her?" The leader asked in a calm voice.

"Yes!" Nevaeh answered without hesitation.

"Damn! Maybe you do have a loyal bone in that nice little body of yours, or is this your girlfriend? I think you two, eat each other out and dildo fuck one another."

"No, she is my best friend. We don't do that shit," Nevaeh answered as she looked over at her wounded friend. "Please, I beg you; just leave her alone, please." Nevaeh wept.

"Nevaeh have you ever have a man before? Did you ever have some real strong dick?" The leader asked as he walked over to her friend with the straight razor opened. Fearing for her friend she answered reluctantly.

"No! I have never been with a man like that." The men chuckled.

Savannah

"To save your friend's life, would you fuck all of us?" The leader asked looking around with a slight smile on his face.
Hearing what he asked, Nevaeh closed her eyes as tears streamed down on her face.

"Yes!" she replied as she took a deep breath and let out a sigh.

"That's good to know. Now tell me, were does Savannah live?"

"She lives in North Carolina somewhere near Laurinburg." The leader took out his cell and made a call. He passed on the information to the person on the other end. He looked back at Nevaeh.

"We're not rapist. Free her friend, she suffered enough." One of the men raised the woman's chin and slit her throat.

"NO! YOU MUTHA-FUCKING BASTARD!" Nevaeh screamed out at the men who held her captive. "You bitch ass mutha-fuckas. You have to tie us up to kill us? You are not men; you're nothing but bitch ass mutha-fuckas. It's six of you men and two of us, you punk ass bastard." Her friend's body was drenched with blood as her head slumped down.

"Now, it's just you, you disloyal bitch," The leader said with a smirk.

"Oh, God! Oh, God! Oh, my God," Nevaeh kept repeating as tears flowed over her pretty face. An associate handed the leader a piece of tape and he placed it over her mouth. Holding the tape over her mouth, he removed a knife from its' sheath and plunged it several times in Nevaeh's stomach and chest. Nevaeh's eyes was wide as if she saw a ghost, veins appeared on her forehead and fear written all over her face. Her screams were muffled as she slumped over on the couch. Nevaeh eyes closed slowly, blood oozed from her wounds as she lay motionless. He took the knife and wiped the blood off it with her hair. He then placed it back in the sheath, while the other men gathered up their gear and left the house, closing the door behind them.

CHAPTER TWENTY-FIVE
"I don't have time to play games"

Later that day, in the afternoon Savannah and her girls said their good bye's to one another. She gave everyone her deepest apology for messing up their vacation. They all agreed if they had to do it all over again they would. *That's what I call true friends*, Savannah said to herself. They looked out for one another and were there for her and her family with no questions asked. Shanna was taking Tee back to New York and Desha was riding back with Savannah to North Carolina, to pick up her car. Before hitting the road, they made a quick stop at Savannah's parents' house. They had a brief conversation on what had happened, while the kids played upstairs. Savannah's parents' employment background with the Central Intelligence Agency never came up and neither one of them volunteered any information about what the other knew. Thirty minutes later everyone hugged and got on the road. At the end of the block, a family was having what looked like a block party. Savannah brought the car to a full stop at the corner stop sign, when this guy walked up to them and motioned for them to lower the window.

"Ladies and children, how is everyone doing?"

"We're good," Desha and Savannah responded.

"My name is Devon, the reason I stopped you was because I just got my dream job and I wanted to share in the celebration with everyone."

"So what is your dream job?" Savannah asked.

"I'm the new publicist for the Washington Wizards."

"Congratulations!"

"Thank you. So come on get some food and hang out for a minute."

Savannah

"We would love to, but we can't. We have a long trip in front of us," Savannah replied.

"Oh, okay. Then maybe next time. Hold on let me give you something for the road." He ran back and opened a red cooler that was underneath a folding table that was on the lawn. He took out something and ran back to the car. Savannah and Desha didn't think nothing of his gesture's because they figured he lived down the street from her parent's in the influential neighborhood, so he must be alright.

"Here are some nutty-butty ice cream cones for the little guys and here is a cup with some ice and a small bottle of Patron." He handed the Patron and cup of ice to Desha.

"What are your names?" He asked with a smile, revealing perfect white teeth.

"I'm Desha and she's Savannah."

"You already know my name."

"It was nice to meet you, Devon, and good luck with your new job." Savannah said. "And thanks for the Patron." Desha added, as she place the cup in the cup holder.

"Well, okay beautiful ladies have a safe trip." He then turned away and began to dance to the music that was playing from the back yard of the house. The boys laughed at the man antics as they drove away.

"I never had Patron Silver before," Desha admitted, as she poured a half of cup before taking a sip. "Wow this is good girl."

"Yeah, it's smooth, isn't it?"

"I'm going to get some good sleep from drinking this." Desha said, with a stupid grin on her face. Savannah giggled.

Just before getting on I-95 south, Savannah received a call from Valerie. They talked briefly, and then she wished Savannah a safe trip back to North Carolina.

"Savannah, that cup of Patron has me against the ropes. I didn't know it had a kick like that," Desha said propping her pillow against the window to rest her head.

"Yeah, girl, it's a smooth drink and it will make you horny too." They both chuckled at the statement.

Brooklen Borne

"Wake me up when you get tired and I'll take over, alright?" Desha words faded as she dozed off into a deep sleep. Savannah looked over at her friend and just smiled as she continued south on I-95.

*****

As they traveled south on Interstate 95, the sun was falling behind the horizon. Savannah looked over at Desha and she was still passed out. She looked in the rear view mirror and her precious cargo was also asleep. She was alone with her thoughts, as she thought about the poem she had read in Essence. *Thank you Lord for your sacrifices of my sins, thank you Lord for forgiveness of my sins, and thank you Lord for saving me from my sins.* A smile came across her face, because for the first time in years, she was finally at peace. Savannah's heart was still cold toward Ricky and made a call to the prison to never let any monies to go back into his commissary.

She looked over at Desha and began to wonder, why she was sleeping so long and then she remembered the cup of Patron Silver Tequila. *At lease she will be well rested for her trip, if she decides to leave right away,* Savannah smiled to herself. They were just about home, when she received a call.

"Hello!" Savannah greeted the caller.

"Don't rush to get home." The unidentified male voice informed her.

"What? Who is this? (A long pause) I don't have time to play games."

"I said don't rush to get home." The unidentified male voice repeated. As she turned the corner onto the block, where she lived, her home exploded right before her eyes. The explosion gushed fire and debris everywhere. The explosion was so loud it shook the car violently. The car came to screeching halt. Savannah couldn't believe what she was seeing. With her mouth wide open and the area where her home once stood engulfed in flame. She was the only one in the car that saw what happened. No one in the car had woken up. She shook Desha and yelled out her children names. She shook Desha again and she leaned over toward Savannah as if she was

Savannah

dead. The only thing that kept her from falling onto Savannah was the seat belt Desha was secured in.

Fear ran through Savannah's body as she unbuckled Desha's seatbelt and turned to her boys. She yelled at them as she shook their limp bodies. They awoke scared, wondering why their mother was franticly shaking them. Savannah looked at them and asked them if they were all right. They both acknowledge they were okay and were fine, she then turned her attention back to Desha. Savannah took her wrist in her hand and checked for a pulse . . . She didn't feel one. *Shit! She can't be dead.* Savannah said to herself fearing the worst.

Tears streamed down her face as she tried to compose herself. Yet her surroundings and everything seemed so surreal. The children began to cry along with her. They kept asking why she was crying and what was wrong with Desha. It was only then that Savannah heard an unidentified male voice in her Bluetooth ear piece.

"Savannah! Savannah, are you there?"

She responded in frustration and in shock. I'm here. Who the hell is this?"

"Bitch, I'm the guy who gave your girl the bottle of Patron. You're lucky I didn't taint your kids' ice cream cones."

"Devon?" She yelled into the earpiece.

"That's me, but that's not my real name."

"So who the hell are you?" She screamed again into the earpiece.

"Don't worry about who I am. I will make your life miserable and then I'm going to take it."

"Mutha-fucka, I may not know who you are, but you can believe on thing. I will hunt you down and gut you like a deer, then set your ass on fire."

There wasn't a response from the man, who had called himself Devon. The line went dead. She tried calling him back, but it was an unknown number. Savannah's children were crying and yelling for her to call 911. Savannah was in a morbid state as she sat there paralyzed. Too much had taken place and she was only one person. She gripped the steering wheel with both hands as her eyes where affixed on her burning home.

People were now showing up at the scene with their cell phones to their ear calling the fire and police department. With all the commotion going on outside, Savannah begged to enter a world of her own. Perhaps one in which she could escape momentarily. She had a single thought so intense, tears flowed uncontrollably from her eyes, as she spoke aloud . . . *Only God Almighty Himself will be able to protect those behind this.*

The End

Coming in 2012
"Savannah's Fury"

Here's a preview...

Silent tears rolled down Savannah's cheeks, as her children held onto her crying uncontrollably. She couldn't believe Desha was dead, as the ambulance drove away with her body to the morgue. Because of a drug kingpin's disregard to human life, people that she love dearly is being taken from her at will. Savannah's world is crumbling around her. She feels lost, scared and almost not knowing what to do.

An hour later, at the morgue, two assistance lifts Desha's body from the gurney onto a stainless steel table, so they could slide her into a coffin freezer. The state examiner is going to perform an autopsy, first thing in the morning; due to the nature of Desha's death. The news of her death went nationwide and is now going to be a high profile case. Finding out how she died was a top priority and the authorities needed to be ready for any questions asked, at the news conference the next day.

"Man, this is a waste of such a beautiful body. I wish I could have had some of this." One of the assistance said, as he looked up and down Desha's lifeless body.

"Look you pervert, just place the sheet over her body and slide her in the freezer." The other assistant instructed.

"I'm just saying, she has a bad ass figure. Look at those tits's man."

"You have some major issues that need to be addressed. Just place the sheet over her. I'm going to get some supplies. I'll be back in a few.

"Alright man, take your time." He replied as he began covering her up. His perversion got the best of him as he slid the sheet towards her breast. He focused on her erect nipples and began to fondle her breast. He was amazed how firm and soft they felt, when all of a sudden Desha reached up and grabbed both wrists. He began to scream in fear. She twisted both wrists breaking them, while throwing him to the floor and straddling him, in one fluent motion.

"Who are you? Where am I?" Desha asked, confused and feeling groggy. She eased up on the pressure of her hand that was covering his mouth, so he could answer.

"I'm an assistant and you are at the morgue. You were brought here about an hour ago. We thought you were dead." He stuttered.

"So you felt me up, because you thought I was dead? You are sick little fucka."

"I'm sorry." He replied still shaking and stuttering from fear.

"Where are my clothes?" She asked with fire in her eyes. He motioned with his head, in the direction of the closet, located in the far corner of the room. She stood up and scurried towards the closet, with her arms crossed, to cover her breast. The assistant sat up positioning himself against the table, watching her every move. He couldn't take his eyes off her, still not believing she was alive.

"Do you have a cell phone and a car?" She snarled at him shivering, as she donned her clothes.

"Yes!" He answered timidly. With his broken wrists pressed against his body for support he answered. "They're in my pocket." She retrieves the items from his white lab coat.

"What kind of car is it? And where's it located?"

"It's a white Honda Accord, located on the P3 level." She was about to leave, when she stopped and came back to him.

"I don't believe you got a job working here. Because, if you have the need to feel up on dead women.....never mind." She became too disgusted to finish her sentence and punched him in the jaw, knocking him out.

She made her way to the parking lot, without incident. Once in the car, she paused for a second before dialing Savannah's number.

Book Club Question

Q. Do you think Savannah, should have let the police handle her situation?

Q. Would Savannah, have succeeded in her mission, without help from Valerie?

Q. Why would Savannah parents trust Nevaeh?

Q. Was Savannah and her crew vigilantes or just a mother, trying to protect her own?

Q. Should Savannah; let the authorities know about the mysterious phone call she received, in reference to her house being blown up?

Made in the USA
Charleston, SC
02 June 2011